MW01687927

Indian Giver

Thomas J. Canter

Kirk House Publishers
Minneapolis, Minnesota

Indian Giver

Thomas J. Canter

Edited by Samantha J. Extance and Karen Walhof

ISBN 13: 978-1-933794-11-2
ISBN 10: 1-933794-11-9

Library of Congress Control Number: 2008935372

Kirk House Publishers, PO Box 390759, Minneapolis, MN 55439
Manufactured in the United States of America

In memory of my loving mother

Lola G. Kelly

The sun was shining directly into the FBI agent's eyes. His head throbbed even more. The sick headache compounded his already weakened physical state. A few gloomy clouds drifted over the vast field in front of him, casting irregular outlines on the ground, making it difficult for him to estimate the distance to his target. Not a good position, he thought. The sighting of his gun might be off because of the poor light conditions. He did not have the luxury of time. In a few moments the plane would take off from the field. He had to stop the man who was about to enter it. The agent did not know if he had the strength to pull the trigger. More importantly, he did not know if he had the courage to shoot the man before him.

His attention was focused on the man about to enter the airplane. The distance was a good 300 meters.

The man was a fugitive wanted by every law enforcement agency in the country. He had stolen a weapon, one that could possibly destroy American society. The entire nation could be thrown into a past century, a time when only the strong could survive. The beads of cold sweat running down his forehead added to his discomfort. This was the most important shot of his life. The world could change overnight if the fugitive got the plane off the ground. Millions of Americans would die of thirst and starvation. There would be no electricity. Hospitals would be useless. After the food on the grocery store shelves was depleted, the shelves would remain empty for many months. The modern day transportation system would cease to function. No fuel, no communications. There would be mass rioting. Gangs would form overnight, killing, raping, and stealing. Countless numbers would attempt to flee the large cities, to escape the unimaginable stench of human corpses, to hide, to find a sanctuary were they and their loved ones could be safe and secure. Each man and woman would be forced to fight to defend what little food they could hoard.

The agent was not a trained sniper. He would have given anything not to be in his present predicament. There was no one else to stop the fugitive, it had to be him. He was still weak from his wounds. The exertion of just getting to this remote area had taken its toll, physically and mentally. He was shaking. The tears running freely down his cheeks from exhaustion, pain, and regret did not help matters. He took up the slack on the trigger and squeezed ever so gently. A split second before the roar of the gun, the target turned his head to look directly at him.

The criminal's instincts, fine-tuned with years of combat experience in the military, sent him diving to the ground when the bullet struck him. The bullet entered just above his left eye, lifting him off the ground and throwing him violently against the wing of the aircraft. As he crumbled slowly to the ground, his thoughts, somewhat jumbled from the incomplete circuits of destroyed brain matter, returned to his past.

As the criminal was falling, he began to see his life pass before his eyes. The sniper, upon seeing the impact of the bullet, began reliving his past as well. The two men lay alone on the small airstrip, one dying and the other so badly injured he could barely move. Mustering up every ounce of strength he could find, the FBI agent began his slow, torturous, and agonizing crawl.

"I'm coming, dad!" he sobbed. "I'm coming. Don't die on me!"

CHAPTER 1

1948: The last memory

The young Indian woman sang softly to the little three-year-old boy as he scurried about the forest locating the brightly colored Easter eggs. Her motherly voice sang with pride in her native Blackfoot tongue: Little warrior, you are the pride of the Blackfoot Nation; all will stand before you and your chieftain ways.

The two of them sat together snuggled under the generous shade of a large oak tree, the soft moss climbed up from a gurgling stream running nearby. It provided a luxurious blanket for them to sit on. This was their special place. At least once a day they went there to lie on the soft grass and look at the clouds as they formed different shapes of animals and birds.

She peeled one of the magic eggs he had found and handed it to him. He insisted she take the first bite. Smiling at him for his generosity, she took a bite and rolled her eyes as she exclaimed that this was the best egg in the whole world. He beamed under her constant love. He had never felt as grown-up as he did at this moment. That morning she had surprised him with a buckskin suit. He sat, caressing the soft deerskin while he admired the intricate detail of bead work on his shirt and moccasins. He had to get up and run, the new footwear feeling light as a feather. She laughed, that wonderful musical laugh, as he ran within range of her arms. She grabbed him and brought him to her in a tight embrace. He squirmed away from her, feeling much too big to be hugged in such a way. The sad look on her face made him change his mind, and he leaped back into her waiting arms amid her soft laughter. She squeezed him tightly. He was happy. His mother was his world. His father would become part of his world in the early evenings.

He heard the old pickup truck several miles before he could see it. It struggled up the old logging trail. Freeing himself from his mother, he ran to the edge of the wood and waited for the truck to pull into the clearing.

He ran to his father who got out of the truck and swooped him in his arms. His father threw him up on his strong shoulders and gave him a piece of candy from his pocket. He could see his mother waiting for them in the doorway. She always waited for her two men to come home together. A big smile crossed her face. His dad lifted him down with one hand. He placed his other arm around his mother and kissed her. He was forgotten in that moment. They were in their own special place, each other's arms. But it wasn't long before they diverted their attention back to him. He was the center of their universe. His days were filled with love and kindness. Life was so good then.

He gave his dad the last colored egg. He had found it just for him! He watched him eat the egg slowly with a solemn expression. After several moments, the egg was pronounced to be the best egg his dad had ever eaten. He went to sleep that night listening to the whippoorwills in the nearby woods, feeling safe, happy, and loved. Tomorrow he and his mother would do some house chores. He liked to help her. He couldn't wait for the next Easter. Next time, he thought just before sleep overcame his tired little body, he would find even more eggs.

He awoke to his mother's singing. He lay in his small bed for a few minutes and listened to her beautiful voice. Getting out of bed, he made his way into the kitchen. "Good morning, little warrior!" She beamed at him in her special way. He took his place at the table, and she brought him a plate of bacon and eggs. The fried eggs had been cooked for his dad who had eaten the white part and saved him the yolk. It was a morning ritual. His mother continued to sing as she went about adding fire wood to the stove, preparing to make a cake. He watched her moving about the kitchen in her graceful manner.

They were standing there in the open doorway of the house—strangers who scared him as he looked up from his breakfast at the kitchen table. Two men, both unshaven and dirty, were staring at his mother with unfamiliar smiles, smiles he had never seen before. He was about to call out to his mother when she turned around and saw them. For a split second, he saw the look of fear cross her face. Then a resolute Indian hardness came over her as she asked the two strangers what they were doing on private property. They walked through the door, neither man saying a word. The one with a blue-checkered shirt and broken teeth slapped him hard with the open palm of his hand. Falling backwards, his head hit the metal frame of the stove. The last sound he would ever hear from his mother was a high-pitched scream. He blacked out.

He awoke, crying from the pain. He could not get his eyes to focus for more than a few seconds before the room began to swim. He felt sick to his stomach. He called for his mother. She did not come. He threw up. He passed out again. He repeated this process numerous times throughout the long day, passing out and waking to call for his mother. He was so thirsty.

In the late afternoon he awoke once more. Moving his head slowly, his eyes cleared enough for him to see his mother lying on the floor next to the door. Her eyes were wide open, her mouth pursed in a shattered scream. He could see blood dried around her throat from the gaping hole. Her dress was pulled up above her waist, exposing her nakedness. He cried for her to help him one more time.

He could not remember very much after that day or the weeks that followed. Pictures and images floated in and out of his brain like an incomplete puzzle. He was in his bed, with his dad tending to him, talking to him about the men and what they looked like and what kind of clothes they were wearing. After a while, he remembered the one with the broken teeth and blue-checkered shirt. His head hurt, and he would get sick from the spinning room. An old Indian woman sat with him, feeding him and making him drink a bitter liquid. He cried for his mother. He cried for his father. Neither came to help him.

His father finally came home. Something was wrong with his arm though. He had it wrapped with a dirty blue-checkered piece of cloth.

"Where's mom?" he asked his father.

"She's gone, son. She's in heaven now, and she can never come back." He cried, demanding his mother. He screamed for his mother. He was too young to understand what heaven was, but he hated it for taking his mother away from him. He screamed and cried in his father's arms until he fell asleep.

CHAPTER 2

August, 1970

Scared? He thought so. How could he not be? After two weeks of training he was about to leap from the C-123 aircraft that was droning loudly in his ears. His first jump. Hopefully, not his last.

Looking around at the other jumpers packed tightly in the aircraft, he could sense their collective fear. Their tense movements and darting eyes reminded him of his combat patrols in Vietnam. He could detect the smell of fear coming from the jumpers sitting next to him; the obnoxious odor was filling the aircraft. True fear has a smell of its own, worse than a rotting tooth smell. It comes from the bile of your stomach and seeps through every pore in the body to erupt in an unexplainable odor, a stench so strong it makes a person gag when forced to inhale it. The poor bastards who jumped into Normandy during World War II must have had a worse case than this, he thought. The one factor that kept driving him for the past two weeks was that there were others who had gone before him. They had gone through the very same training and survived. He would too. Regardless of how difficult the training or how scared he was, he would complete his jump training.

Some of the soldiers were sleeping but not from boredom as one might expect on a long flight. They were allowing their bodies to shut down as a way of coping with the unknown. Most of the jumpers were facing death for the first time in their young lives. Looking at the faces sitting across from him, he realized he was several years older than most of the thirty men packed inside the aircraft. Perhaps, he thought, I am more scared than they are. I have lived longer. He was a Vietnam veteran and had faced death on several different occasions. Nothing, compared to some soldiers he had known. Yet enough to pray he would never have to see any more.

He was not a big man—five foot seven, one hundred and forty pounds of solid muscle. Thick, black, wavy hair sat atop a face with a slight brown complexion, and there was a slight Oriental shape around his dark green eyes. Most assumed he was Oriental. He was not. His mother had been a full-blooded Blackfoot Indian, a fact he was extremely proud to admit and had fought many times to defend.

He had to urinate, being in the parachute harness for the past three hours. Five cups of coffee for breakfast and his own fear had quadrupled the effects to as where his kidneys felt they might explode if not relieved soon. Suddenly, the jumpmaster opened the side door of the aircraft, bringing in a wave of much-needed fresh air and a new sense of urgency to all first-time jumpers inside. He yawned, not from boredom but another unexplainable defense of the body when overwhelmed with fear. Several others were doing the same, and it caused a ripple effect throughout the aircraft.

Over the roar of the engines, the jumpmaster gave his first command. "TWENTY MINUTES!"

His heart started racing a little faster. The well-known butterflies in the pit of his stomach started climbing higher. Nothing to do in twenty minutes but wait for the next command. He caught a glimpse of what seemed like miniature treetops as the plane made a slight bank, exposing the ground through the open door.

"TEN MINUTES!" The heartbeat within his chest reverberated loudly in his ears.

"SIX MINUTES!" The time for action, he unhooked his safety belt and felt a slight disconnection from the aircraft, one that he was not sure he wanted to have.

The jumpmaster began to give a series of rapid commands. The jumpers knew all the commands by heart and reacted without pausing to think.

"GET READY! OUT BOARD PERSONNEL STAND UP!" As if in one body, the entire mass of soldiers came to their feet, somewhat unsteady, as the aircraft floor swayed from side to side beneath them.

"HOOKUP! IN BOARD PERSONNEL STAND UP!" The remaining jumpers struggled to gain an upright position as the aircraft rocked beneath their feet.

"HOOKUP!" The next command from the jumpmaster came to him loud and clear. He fumbled briefly with the static line hook as he worked it free from his reserve parachute handle. He snapped it into place on the cable suspended directly over his head. He checked the static line of the jumper in front of him, insuring it was in the correct place, a second ahead of the jumpmaster's next command.

"CHECK STATIC LINE. CHECK EQUIPMENT. SOUND OFF FOR EQUIPMENT CHECK!" He received a familiar slap on his right ass cheek from the jumper standing behind him. "OK!" was yelled into his right ear. He in turn gave the same slap and "OK" to the jumper in front of him, this being repeated by each man until the jumper standing in front of the jumpmaster, the one closest to the open door, pointed his hand with his fingers extended and joined to yell, "ALL OK!"

The jumpmaster braced his hands on either side of the door frame and slowly leaned out of the aircraft. The back blast of the propeller tugged furiously at his uniform, trying to pull him from his perch and hurl him towards the earth. Someday I will do that, he thought. The jumpmaster was looking in a 360-degree arch for other aircraft and for the brightly marked panels on the ground. I hope it is easier than it looks, he thought, as butterflies stirred nervously with excitement in his stomach.

Pulling himself back inside the aircraft, the jumpmaster gave his next series of commands. "ONE MINUTE! STAND IN THE DOOR!" All the jumpers moved forward. The one closest to the door planted his feet and assumed a good exit position. His eyes looked straight ahead, his hands placed on the outside skin of the aircraft, his knees bent, ready to spring up and out on command. His head swam when he got a glimpse of the ground below. Sure is a long way, he thought as he stared down at the trees 1500 feet below him.

"GO!" the jumpmaster yelled as he slapped the first and then each proceeding jumper on the rump. Two weeks of the same command, the same slap on the right butt cheek as he made the practiced exits from the thirty-four-foot tower. It had built a natural instinct to jump and a large bruise on his hip.

Each jumper, without hesitation, exited the aircraft and disappeared. The same procedure went on with two-second intervals between each jumper. When it was finally his turn, the training took over the fear of the unknown. The butterflies disappeared as he slapped his palms onto the outside skin of the aircraft. "GO!" The command from the jumpmaster rang loud in this ear. He intentionally made his exit just ahead of the jumpmaster's hand to escape the full impact of the slap on his bruised ass cheek.

All parts of his first airborne exit came to him in slow motion. He felt the mixture of fuel and hot wind from the plane's engine blasting hot against his face. It made it impossible to breathe from its sheer force. His eyes took in brief glimpses of the ground over the tops of his army boots. His body turned slowly until his back was toward the departing wings of the plane. He felt his parachute open. The opening shock was not as bad as he had feared. He looked up to see a full canopy above his head. A sense of wonder and awe overtook him and stayed with him as saw in what he thought must be the most adrenaline-producing sight in the world. He could see the curvature of the earth. The wind caressed his face with a gentle embrace of welcome. The trees below looked like miniature models placed neatly on the ground by a passing giant. He was a giant!

The sudden quiet left his ears ringing. His eyes, still watery from the prop blast of the aircraft, took in the jumpers near him. Several of them were yelling, "AIRBORNE!" as they floated beneath a parachute that strained under their weight. Looking down he could see the ground swaying beneath his feet. He felt completely disconnected from the earth and yet surprised that he did not feel the effects of height. There was no sensation other than just sitting in his harness. He could see the ground slowly moving toward him as though it were reaching upward with invisible fingers to reclaim its loss of gravity over him. Doing as he was trained, he looked around for other jumpers. He could see several hitting the ground and estimated his distance above the ground to be 200 feet.

He started going over his pre-landing checks and could feel the familiar bite of fear rising in him again. What if I break a leg or my back? He started talking to himself: feet and knees together, knees slightly bent, toes pointed slightly downward. The ground was coming toward him faster now. Was he falling too fast? A quick glance above confirmed the canopy was full of air. Too fast? His body tensed, not a good thing to do. He hit the ground hard as he attempted a parachute-landing fall, a PLF.

He felt the shock as his hips and head slammed onto the ground. No broken bones, just another bruise like one of the many that he sustained during the past two weeks of jump school. Getting up as fast as he could, he collapsed his parachute to prevent the air from re-inflating the canopy and dragging him along the ground. As he unhooked his harness, the words, "Thank you, Great Spirit," whispered from his lips. After rolling and stuffing his parachute into the kit bag, he started the half-mile walk to the parachute turn-in point. The dry grass, burned by the relentless Georgia sun, crunched under his boots and sent up small spirals of dust. The dust quickly covered his spit-shined boots and clung to his sweat-soaked fatigues.

He could hardly contain his excitement. Due to the excellent weather conditions, they were going to jump twice today. He was ready!

He knew the fear would not be as severe as the first jump now that the unknown was a matter of the past. Tomorrow, he was not sure. He was not afraid of death itself. No, his fear was one of severe injury that would keep him in a wheelchair for the rest of his life, or worse. One down, four more jumps to go, and he would have his wings— a badge of honor among soldiers throughout the world. For him this was just a stepping stone to his final goal. After jump school he was going to Fort Bragg, North Carolina, for Special Forces Training. Civilians called Special Forces soldiers Green Berets because of the distinctive headgear they wore.

The United States had what he considered to be a substandard army. It was torn apart by politics, inept officers, and non-commissioned officers, and drugs were becoming common throughout all branches of the service. The lifestyle of the '60s generation and the increasing numbers of young men called up for the draft to support the Vietnam War were the primary culprits for the increase in drugs in the service. But he blamed the poor leadership he had witnessed during the past four years in the military as the real perpetrator. He had just completed a tour of duty as a drill instructor at Fort Leonard Wood, Missouri, where he had worked with some professional soldiers for the first time since his enlistment in the Army. They were the reason he volunteered for Special Forces training. He wanted to serve with real soldiers, men he could count on to do their jobs.

He recalled his welcome home from Vietnam. Landing at Fort Lewis, Washington, he was sized for a new uniform. He was served a steak dinner while the uniform was being tailored. By the time he had finished eating, his uniform, complete with awards and decorations, was waiting for him. Within hours of his return to the States, he was on a plane headed home. He had a stopover in Chicago, his first experience with the anti-war demonstrators he had heard about while overseas. The anger and pure hatred these people displayed almost overwhelmed him. The attitude of those opposing the war now focused on the soldiers returning. Young girls no more than fifteen or sixteen years old had formed a line and were directing their anger toward any soldier wearing a uniform. They were calling the young soldiers criminals and murderers. Several of the angrier girls spat on him as he walked past them. This caught him completely by surprise. He had been informed by the new soldiers arriving in Vietnam that many American people were now opposed to the war, but he had not been told that they were treating their own soldiers in this manner.

A young man with dirty, stringy hair and a very thin beard stood behind several of the teenage girls. Looking over the top of his rose-colored sunglasses that rested halfway down a large nose, he asked as he passed by, "How many babies did you kill?" He could see the fear in the eyes that sat behind the small round glasses and dismissed him. Had there been a glimmer of hatred or challenge in those eyes, he may have gone through the crowd of young girls and killed him. He was unworthy, just another coward. He had seen his type in Vietnam, boys so scared they would inflict an injury on themselves to go home or turn to drugs to deny their surroundings.

Baby killer? Instantly he thought of Mamma Son who used to sell them Cokes for a dollar a can. They were was cold and worth the buck. Her five-year-old daughter sat beside her on the dirt road, smiling at him in a shy, bashful way, as the two of them rolled a Coke can over a block of ice. He saved his C-ration candy to give to this little girl whenever he and his squad stopped by for a Coke. She was small even by Vietnamese standards. Her father was dead, killed three years before fighting the North Vietnamese army. Baby killer? He would never forget one day when his squad stopped to buy a Coke. He could hear Mamma Son crying as only a mother can when her child has died. The mournful sound came from inside the hut in which they lived. It was not much of a house, just a mixture of discarded artillery boxes and cardboard from the Army C-rations, assembled and held together with wire over a dirt floor. He stepped inside, with the premonition that he would never be the same. Mamma Son sat on the dirt floor holding the little girl's lifeless body to her chest. Blood was everywhere, smeared on the mother and covering the little girl's entire body. Mamma Son was gently rocking back and forth, saying words he could not understand. Gently, he sat beside her and carefully pulled the little girl away from her, far enough to see that she had been cut from the base of her neck to her vagina, and all her inner body parts had been removed. The Vietcong had stopped by earlier that morning and left this as a lesson for anyone who would sell Cokes to American soldiers. Baby killer? After all this time, he was still unable to drink a Coke.

He had reached the parachute turn-in point and was relieved to be in the company of others, relieved that the distraction had brought him back to reality. His mind could forget the war for only a short time, wandering into the past like this after stress or an adrenaline rush. He still had nightmares. He often woke up in the middle of the night with a cold sweat soaking him and his bedding.

Dropping off his chute, he hopped onto one of the waiting trucks for a thirty-minute ride back to Fort Benning. The young soldiers were loud and funny, burning off the excess of adrenaline that flowed through their bodies. After lunch, he was suited up and going through another pre-flight and jump briefing. This time he would exit a C-141, a large jet aircraft, instead of the antiquated C-123. There was no jumping out of this plane. All one had to do was walk at an angle, until you were close enough to the door to be sucked out. He found this jump did not have the intensity as his first one, although the butterflies were still there and the constant worry of a possible entanglement with another jumper was in the back of his mind. When he made his exit, his body position was not as tight as it should have been. The outside forces spun him around and gave him a close view of the tail section of the aircraft. The plane slowly moved away from him, spitting a jumper from the door every second. Fantastic! he thought as he slowly floated downward.

The Georgian sun was low enough in the horizon to give an almost mystical appearance of the surrounding jumpers. A good PLF. A "Thank you, Lord," under his breath. He had made a habit of saying, "Great Spirit and/or Lord" to honor both parents. After a short ride back to Fort Benning, they were released for the remainder of the day now already growing dim. He felt he had earned his money that day and with just three more jumps, he was that much closer to Fort Bragg.

Entering the barracks, he thought about his options for the evening. After chow, he would walk over to the enlisted men's club, have a beer to celebrate, and listen to his fellow jumpers talk of their exploits, knowing only a soldier could take a serious situation and turn it into the most hilarious story. Then he would turn in for a good night's rest. He stretched out on his bunk for just a few minutes rest and was almost instantly asleep. His good time would have to wait for another day. The day's events had sapped all his strength, and he slept soundly for the first time in weeks.

He awoke the next morning to the familiar noises of an Army barracks: the steady hum of buffers cleaning the main hallway, yells coming from the showers, the water fluctuated between hot and cold with each flush of the dozen toilets in constant use. Sitting up and putting his feet on the floor, he realized he had never felt so tired. Even after ten hours of sleep every muscle was sore and he could feel the bruises as he shifted his weight.

"Good morning!" said a voice from the only other bunk in the room. His roommate, a tall thin sergeant from Georgia, had just completed a tour of duty in Germany. He had requested jump school in the hopes of being stationed at Fort Benning which was closer to his home. "When I came in last night, you were snoring so loud I couldn't fall asleep till past midnight."

"Sorry," he replied, not meaning it. His roommate had kept him awake a few nights doing the very same thing.

"I've been thinking," said the tall, thin man, "that if I don't get stationed here, I might go to Drill Sergeant School. How did you like it?" He asked the short man sitting on his bunk who was still in his uniform and boots from the day before.

"Ok, if you don't mind putting up with the best and worst that humanity has to offer, if you don't mind going without sleep for several nights or missing meals on a daily basis. It's supposed to be good for your career. Guess I will find out in a couple of years."

Getting off his bunk, he could see the first streaks of sunlight breaking through the window. The sky was orange and purple, smitten with dark, enraged clouds that were gathering slowly in the distance.

"Sure hope we get a jump in today," he said with mixed emotions. He stretched, his muscles responding gratefully for the attention given to them. "One jump today, one tonight, and finish up tomorrow. What are you going to do when we graduate?" he asked his tall, lanky roommate.

"Dunno," said the sergeant, taking the conversation in a direction that was heavy on his mind. "Maybe I'll take your advice and see a doctor, but I think it was just a strain of some kind. I've stopped leaking, and the pain when I piss ain't as bad."

A slow anger came over him as he listened to his roommate's self-evaluation, knowing the turmoil he must be dealing with inside. His roommate had spent two weeks leave with his wife on his return from Germany. Not having been with anyone other than his wife, he was now displaying all the symptoms of a sexually-transmitted disease. His advice when he first learned of his roommate's condition had been medical rather than personal. He knew first hand how the sergeant was feeling. Coming home after a year in Vietnam, he had found his girlfriend three months pregnant. It was devastating to him. Her cards and letters had never given him any indication she was seeing someone else. After she was sure he would not stay with her, she quickly married the guitar player she had been living with while he was overseas.

He had spent a lot of time blaming himself for his girlfriend's actions. He knew no one could have given him advice on what to do. It was something he had to work out alone. He had just gotten over sleepless nights the past year. There was nothing he could tell his roommate. He would have to work it out the best way for himself. Once he came to grips with the fact that his wife had been cheating on him, he would either choose to stay or go. It was his choice.

The hallways were beginning to come alive, and the noise level was increasing. All the future paratroopers were awake by now even though there was still a full hour before chow. It was another hour before his first cup of coffee. He thought about having a cigarette but decided to wait a little while longer. Going to his wall locker he laid out a fresh, starched uniform on his bunk. Stripping out of the sweaty, dirt-stained uniform from the day before, he slid his feet into a pair of shower shoes. After wrapping a towel around his waist, with his shaving kit in hand, he made off to the large latrine at the end of the hall.

A young private greeted him by throwing up in the toilet. He had obviously partied a little too long the night before. Another soldier was sitting on the toilet next to him, running through a list of things not to think of when your stomach is upset: fried bacon smell from the mess hall, raw oysters, and runny eggs. A look of pure delight reflected from the face and eyes of the curator at his friend's misery. Best friends, he thought to himself as he carefully stepped over some barf that had splattered onto the floor. An enemy would have more compassion.

He stepped into the shower with the sounds of another gut-retching dry heave and laughter in the background. He turned the water on as hot as he could possibly stand it. He allowed the hot steam to pound his tired body. The bruise on his hip from his first PLF was larger than his hand, but it seemed ok. He could handle the pain so as not to bring scrutiny from a black hat and run the risk of being ordered to go on sick call, then facing the possibility of being recycled. His feet were in fair condition. Running five miles with boots on had done some damage, but the blisters were not hurting as bad now that the hot water soothed them. A loud fart erupted from just outside the shower. It sounded like a wet whoopee cushion.

"Oh shit!" moaned a new voice with more than dismay. "I just crapped myself!" After he had dried off and placed the towel around his waist, he passed the soldier who was muttering to himself as he was removing his boots and fatigues. "Last time I eat at that fuckin' place!"

The soldier who had been barfing stood at the sink and splashed cold water on his face. His buddy was long gone now that the fun had stopped.

Stopping two sinks away he brushed his teeth, cupping his hands under the waterspout to rinse his mouth. Turning the water to hot, he soaked his face and applied shaving cream. Glancing over at the sick soldier again confirmed his first impression. The private was too young to shave but maybe once a week if that. This brought back memories of himself when he was eighteen and could pass inspection without the daily worry of shaving. Lucky bastard, he thought. Then he changed his mind as he recalled memories of how embarrassed he had been when older men had teased him. His Indian blood did not allow for a full crop of beard, but he had just enough growth of sparse hair to look shabby if he did not shave.

Going back to his room, he dried his feet off and got dressed. There was something that always came over him whenever he put on a fresh uniform. He immediately knew he was a soldier and a damn good one at that. Lacing up his other pair of highly-shined boots, he quickly added a fresh coat of polish to the ones he had worn the day before. Walking outside, he moved over to the group of non-commissioned officers and lit up his first cigarette of the day. Being more of a listener than a talker, he stood back and enjoyed humor only a GI can have.

"Man I was so scared yesterday you couldn't drive a ten-penny nail up my ass with a twenty-pound sledgehammer," a young buck sergeant remarked.

"I actually got a hard on!" said another. "I heard you could be so scared that this would happen, but I didn't believe it."

"Were you scared?" said one corporal to his tall, lanky friend.

"Nah," came the reply. "I always smell a little like shit."

"A sign of a true ass kisser!" Someone else interrupted the speaker before he could finish his own self-imposed degrading remark.

"Fuck you! You ass wipe!" was the lanky sergeant's only reply.

Chuckling under his breath, he put his cigarette in the number ten coffee can mounted on a pole. Large red letters on the can read, "Butts only." Having heard enough, he headed over to the mess hall to eat breakfast. Coming out fifteen minutes later he stepped over a green slimy hawker some inconsiderate bastard had spat onto the sidewalk. Why couldn't they have taken two steps to spit in the grass? Reaching the barracks he still had ten minutes to kill before the morning formation. Being an ex-drill sergeant and the senior ranking non-com, he had been placed in charge of the company formations, taking roll call and marching the 200-plus men to the training areas.

Soldiers were milling around. Some had started to form into their squads when they saw him approaching. All of them were anxious to get the day started. Walking into the orderly room, he was given a "Good morning" by the sleepy-eyed charge of quarters who muttered, "I didn't get much sleep last night trying to find a bunk for some of the drunks."

"Anyone picked up by the MPs?" he asked as he scanned the C.Q.'s report.

"One Marine was beat up pretty good off post. Hope they recycle the loud-mouth fucker."

All branches of the service came to Benning for jump school. It seemed as though the Marines were given more harassment for their obnoxious behavior and holier-than-thou attitude toward the other branches. He never experienced this type of attitude from the Marines that had been in combat. The new recruits fresh out of boot camp were the ones the other branches of the military could not tolerate. There had been at least one fight after duty hours each day for the past three weeks.

Looking over the C.Q.'s report he found a total of twenty-seven injuries from the previous day's jump—eleven jumpers with broken or sprained ankles, one possible back injury, and the rest with mild to severe bruises. He did not recognize any of the names, so they were just numbers to him. Going outside he stood on the steps so that he could look over the formation which had formed while he had been inside the company headquarters.

"FALL-IN!" said his drill sergeant's voice loud and clear in the morning air. As if in one body, the 200-plus men snapped to attention.

"Report!" he commanded.

"First platoon all present and accounted for!" A salute. "Second platoon all present and accounted for!" After receiving the same from third and fourth platoons, he took his roster back inside.

"No AWOLs to hold you up, so have a good day off," he said to the C.Q. and returned to his formation.

"Right face!" he bellowed at the top of his lungs, "Forward. March!" As one, the company moved out in step. He called cadence for a while. He enjoyed listing to the 200 feet smack in unison on the pavement in perfect timing. As they warmed up and became more alert, he sang a cadence song and could tell by the energetic sound of loud feedback they were all motivated and ready for the day.

"Ain't no use in looking down. Ain't no discharge on the ground. Ain't no use in going home. Jodie got your girl and gone! Am I right or wrong?"

"You're right!"

"Are we going strong?"

"We're strong!"

"Sound off!"

"One-two."

"Sound off!"

"Three-four."

"Bring it on down!"

"One-two-three-four. One-two—three-four!"

The day's events passed quickly, drawing parachutes and loading onto a C-130, a four-engine aircraft that flew much smoother than the old C-123. A good jump, and number three was out of the way and down the tubes. After a quick trip back to the barracks for chow, they were given a long break. The next jump would be a night jump in full combat gear. As he lay on his bunk in his room, he heard the first spatters of rain tapping softly on his window. "God, please don't let the jump be canceled." He knew the same prayer was on everyone else's mind. A wicked downpour erupted, blocking the view of the barracks next to his. And just as sudden, it slowed to a fine drizzle. Within minutes it was completely gone, leaving the hot Georgia sun to evaporate the puddles on the pavement in clouds of steam.

A collective sigh of relief could be heard up and down the barracks as the final drops of rain disappeared. The dark thunderclouds moved away, angry at being unwelcome by so many disgruntled voices. Time passed too quickly this time and before he was mentally ready he was once again standing in the door of a C-130. With the familiar word, "GO!" ringing in his ears and a hard slap on his ass, he was floating in the air. A few bicycle pumps with his legs allowed the twist he had in his suspension lines to undo itself, and he floated downward effortlessly. It was a soft landing just like the instructor had promised, "You can't see the ground so your body won't be as tense when you hit the ground," the instructor had informed them. After dropping off his chute and equipment, he looked at his watch, 2230 hours. A quick calculation, and he determined that after the ride back and a quick shower he would be in bed by 0100. All in all he thought the day had gone really well.

The next morning he awoke to voices outside his barracks window. He lay there listening to two young privates involved in a deep philosophical discussion. "I just can't do it, man. I've never been so scared in my life. Something tells me, if I jump today, it will be my last. I keep having the same dream that I will crash and burn. . . ."

"You have to go through with it, man," his friend interrupted him. "You've come all this way. No way am I going to let you quit now.

Besides, how can you face your unit when you get back after terminating jump status?"

"Screw them, man! They don't give a fuck about me. All they want is some asshole to fill a jump slot. I'm not even worried about losing a promotion over this. Hell, I won't be eligible to make sergeant for at least a year and a half."

His friend, at a loss for words, suddenly struck on the one idea that could change his friend's mind, "Hey, man! So what if you crash and burn! This is your fifth and final jump. Do you know what that means? You would get buried with silver jump wings on your chest!"

Silence. Then the voice of the one contemplating terminating his jump status said, "Say, you know, you're right! I never looked at it that way." This was followed by more silence, as the soldier pictured his friends and relatives standing by his open casket, the many eyes of his loved ones full of tears and yet beaming with pride at the young trooper who lay in blissful eternity. Isn't he handsome in his dress green uniform? All the adoring worshipers would whisper about the coveted jump wings he had earned so bravely.

Suddenly the soldier said to his friend with renewed courage, "You're right, man! Let's go get this goat fuck over with. Thanks, buddy! I never thought of it like that!"

He lay back on his bunk and lit a cigarette, smiling to himself. How young and foolish—and how necessary to have them so in order to face death! Airborne soldiers are the finest soldiers on the planet. They are also just a little touched in the head. Present company exempt, of course. The airborne image is courage, soldiers who are ready to put their lives on the line time and again. The good soldiers he had served with were either dead or maimed for life. They all had one thing in common, he realized. They were young. Most of them, like the young private in the latrine, did not have to shave.

The fifth and final jump went off without a hitch. Clear sky and a soft breeze—a perfect PLF. He felt a great deal of pride as the commanding officer in charge of the airborne training school pinned his wings on his shirt pocket and shook his hand. He congratulated him before moving on down the line. The formation took place on the drop zone. There were no fancy speeches or fancy parades, just a shiny pair of jump wings and a firm handshake. He was calling cadence as they entered the company area. The men's responce was so loud, it shook the windows in the buildings.

"You had a good home when you left!"

"You're right!"

"Your ma was there when you left!"

"You're right!"

"Your pa was there when you left!"

"You're right!"

"Your girl was there when you left!"

"You're right!"

"Your eyes were bright. Your ass was tight. Your balls were swinging from left to right!"

"Sound off!"

"One-two."

"Sound off!"

"Three—four."

"Bring it on down "

"One-two—three-four!"

Upon his return to the barracks, he turned in all of his equipment to the supply room. After signing out of the orderly room, he made his way to his van. He was somewhat amused as he came up behind two young Marines talking in low tones, but loud enough for him to hear. "Man, this is by far the hardest training I've ever had."

Tossing his duffel bag into the back of his van, he lit a Raleigh and stood looking around the parking lot. It had been a tough and demanding three weeks. He was grateful for the professional and realistic training. Pulling out of the parking lot, he drove by the 250-foot towers. He watched the next generation of jumpers floating down. He didn't know or care if he would ever return to Fort Benning, Georgia. He did know one thing: Since his arrival here, his life had changed. . . hopefully for the better.

CHAPTER 3

Fort Bragg was larger than any military post he had served on. A freeway was under construction in order to move the thousands of soldiers and civilians on and off post. It reminded him of a large city with the exception of the obvious military order and cleanliness. He had spent the night off post in a motel. He drove around to get his bearings and observe the nightlife. He drove aimlessly, since he didn't know anyone yet. He found a shopping mall, a few topless bars, and numerous restaurants. A pleasant surprise awaited him: The civilian establishments greeted him with respect and dignity. He knew they were aware he was in the military; even his civilian clothes could not hide his GI haircut. Yet he was treated like everybody else, not the usual "give me your money and get the hell out" attitude he had experienced at Fort Leonard Wood where he was a drill instructor.

After a good meal of steak and potatoes, he drove back to his motel room and relaxed on the bed. He enjoyed the solitude after living in a barracks with 200 men for the past month. Although he liked people and being around them, there would eventually come a time when he had to get away. He did this by camping or backpacking into remote areas he had never been before. He could stay for days at a time, perfectly content to read a book or watch the animals playing. The forest was his friend. There were many spirits there. He always felt a small amount of regret when his time or food ran out, and he was once again forced to return to the rat race.

Looking at the clock on the wall, he allowed his mind to wonder until an image of his dad filtered through. A warm feeling came over him as he thought about the old man. He missed him. He had tried without success to talk his dad into moving in with him and traveling around the country from one post to another. His dad would not leave the old house the two of them had lived in all these years.

"I'm too old, son. Just be a burden on you, and I ain't a'gonna do it." But he knew the real reason that kept his dad living in the old house was the memory of his mother. She had died in that old house when he was only four years old. His dad had never remarried and had never even had a girlfriend when he was growing up. He did not have one now as far as he knew. He's not willing to leave mom, he speculated.

He thought back to his childhood. In some respects it had been very difficult, growing up without a mother and doing without the little things only mothers know and do. He had to do his own laundry, and his clothes had to last him for as long as possible. So he took special care to avoid getting them dirty or torn, a habit that stayed with him even now. He couldn't stand to be dirty or wear old clothes.

He missed his mom, more so now than when he was as a young boy. He could remember a few things about her: her sweet voice as she sang to him so lovely in her native Blackfoot language, her smile, the blackberry pie she baked on that old wood-burning cook stove, her fried chicken—he had yet to find anyone who could come close to hers. She allowed him to help her do laundry on the old washing machine. He remembered getting his hand stuck in the old wringer, the walks in the forest together, the flowers she picked for him, the set of new clothes she had hand-stitched for him on that Easter so long ago—his first set of buckskins, made from deer skins she had bleached white. She had showed him the tanning process from beginning to end, and she had explained each step of the bleaching process to him. Her little warrior, she had called him as he strutted around feeling self important, the buckskins soft and wonderful against his body.

He would never forget his mother on that Easter, his last fond memory of her while she was still alive. He could still hear her laughter as he scurried around the yard finding all those wonderful, colored eggs, and her constant praise and amazement on how many eggs he had found. She always made him feel so special. The two of them sat down under the large old tree with the soft moss beneath it. They ate their eggs in the shade, and she told him again how delicious they were. It was his last fond memory of the two of them together, because before the next Easter came, she was dead.

0800 hours. He was in uniform, outside the in-processing building waiting for it to open. He wanted to be the first in line so that he could get through it as quickly as possible. But he knew from past experience it would be an all day thing. Several other soldiers were sitting in their cars, listening to radios or talking to their wives. Some of the women looked extremely overweight. He wondered why they allowed themselves to get into such poor condition. For some reason military wives, after having several kids, seemed to put on weight and keep it. This was not true in all cases, he knew, but it did seem to run more predominantly in the enlisted ranks.

He had thought about becoming an officer, but he enjoyed working with the soldiers on a more personal level than he would have been able to do if he were an officer. The money was tempting, but he believed he would not be as content with the job and the added responsibility.

A thin-looking older woman who gave him a pleasing smile and a cheerful "Good morning" unlocked the door. With briefcase in hand he reported to station number one. He gave the young girl behind the desk a copy of his orders which said at the top of the page, "Assigned to USAJFKMI" (United States Army John F. Kennedy Institute of Military Instruction).

"So, you're going to be a snake eater!" she said with a smile.

"Guess so." He wasn't able to get over his bashfulness around females. Polite conversation always made him somewhat uneasy. He was afraid of looking foolish.

"Good luck!" she said before she directed him to the next station. He spent the morning hours being shuffled from one station to the next. To his surprise, he was finished just before 1100 hours. He was given directions on how to find the billets in which he would be living. A short fifteen-minute drive brought him to a section of Fort Bragg that was still comprised of the old World War II style wooden barracks. So this is how the best soldiers in the Army live, he mused. Parking his van next to the orderly room in the space reserved for visitors, he went inside and was greeted by a sharp-looking specialist wearing glasses with thick lenses.

"Good morning, sergeant! Are you sure you're in the right place?"

"Yup, guess so," he replied as he looked around a very neat but spartan office.

"The first sergeant will speak with you in a few minutes. Help yourself to a cup of coffee," said the clerk.

He poured a cup of the thick brew thinking how it would give him heartburn if he drank the whole cup, a lesson he had learned as a private while pulling guard duty all night. Army coffee, black, rich, and strong, has kept many a soldier awake with severe stomach pain. Heartburn was the worst thing you could possibly have when you had to stay awake all night, and there was no place available to purchase antacid tablets.

Stepping outside the door of the orderly room, he lit a cigarette and had taken several puffs when the first sergeant came outside and introduced himself. It was an awkward situation for a moment. He tried to hold the coffee and cigarette in his left hand and shake the hand being offered with his right. This seemed to amuse the first sergeant. He chuckled slightly under his breath. He pulled out a pack of smokes and lit one up himself. Looking up at the sky, the first sergeant said, "This would be a good day for a jump."

"Sure would." He put out his cigarette between his finger and thumb and placed the butt in his pocket. He stood looking at the first sergeant. He wasn't a tall man.

As though reading his mind, the first sergeant laughed. "About ninety percent of all the men in Special Forces are made up of men about our size or close to it. Anyone over six feet tall doesn't stick around very long. All the John Waynes leave after about a year, and we seem to just want to hang around. Come on into my office, and bring your coffee." He walked through the door. Sitting in the chair offered him, he was surprised by the next question. "Have you had any broken bones or serious illnesses?"

"Collarbone. Eighth-grade football."

"That may prevent you from making it through phase one training. Depends on you. Has anyone explained to you what you're in for?"

"I heard I would be running a lot with a rucksack."

"That's about it," said the first sergeant with a slight smile. "Care to tell me why you volunteered for this training?"

Taking a deep breath, he started to speak slowly. He did not know if he could convey the thoughts and feelings that brought him to this phase of his life. He told the first sergeant about his tour of duty in Vietnam, the lives he saw destroyed because of drugs, and the frustration he felt trying to lead men who refused to be led. He was tired of inept NCOs and officers that seemed incapable of making a decision or the courage to enforce discipline. How the racial tension found throughout all the units in the regular Army made it nearly impossible for an NCO, black or white, to correct a soldier of another color without the word "prejudice" being thrown at him.

He finished up with his explanation of wanting to work with men he could trust. He thought Special Forces to be the one place left in the Army where he could work as a professional soldier. He wanted to work with men he could depend on in combat. He sat quietly after this, afraid everything he had said may have come across as corny.

The first sergeant looked at him for a few minutes and slowly nodded his head. "Understood," he replied. Then in a louder voice he called the clerk into his office. "Show the sergeant his room, then escort him over to the supply room and help him draw his gear."

After shaking the first sergeant's hand, he was led out by the clerk. The voice of the first sergeant came trailing after them, "Formation out front at 0500 hours!"

"Roger!" he said in a loud voice over his shoulder.

"Seems like a decent guy."

"One of the best," said the clerk. He added in a voice full of respect, "He's been to Nam for three tours."

After drawing his basic issue of boots, rucksack, and field gear; the two of them headed towards his barracks. Glancing at the clerk's thick eyeglasses, he asked him, "How did you make it through training with such poor eyesight?"

The clerk responded in a sad voice, "I've never been through SF training for that very reason."

"But you wear a beret."

The clerk took off his beret and pointed to the thin strip of material sewn on the front. "This is called a candy strip. Shows I'm assigned to this unit, but I am not Special Forces-qualified, like all truck drivers, clerk typists, or parachute riggers. Our job is to get all the little things done so you can concentrate on your job. You can tell who has been through the training by just looking at the beret. It has a whole flash and it looks like a shield. See? Mine just has the bottom one-half inch of the flash."

"Doesn't that cause confusion with other units?"

"You bet!" said the clerk with a smile. "Especially with the civilians. I get laid a lot because girls think I'm a Green Beret. Hope you don't mind, but someone has to stay back and take care of the women while you guys are gone."

"What about the first sergeant?"

"He's the real thing, been shot up so bad he can't hang on an A-team, so he runs the support company here. You'll be here for about a week, more in-processing to do. A final physical and then you'll be sent out to Camp McCall to start phase one of your training. It's only a month long, but more than half of the guys going out there don't last over two weeks. Wish you luck!"

The clerk left him in his room with his thoughts. He sat down on his bunk and digested everything the clerk had told him. A small nagging uneasiness came over him. Would he be one of those to return early from Camp McCall?

With nothing to do, he set out to explore more of the post. He found the PX and decided to do some emergency shopping. He grabbed five cartons of Raleigh cigarettes and some toiletries. Selecting the shortest line to check out, he wondered if his luck with checkout lines had changed. It seemed to him that he always picked the wrong line, and he watched the one he opted out of usher customer after customer through. True to form, as his turn finally came at the checkout, the cashier told him he would have to wait while they switched cashiers since she was now off the clock. He didn't mind this time. A pretty redhead moved gracefully up to the counter to replace the cashier. As she ran her fingers over the cash register, he looked for a ring or any sign indicating she was married or taken. Seeing none, he tried to strike up a conversation with her. "You sure could do me a favor."

"What's that?" she asked.

"I'm new here in town, and I don't know anyone or my way around. How about we have dinner when you get off and. . ."

"Sorry, I'm already married."

"F–Forgive me I didn't know." He stammered, feeling the blood flow through his cheeks.

"That's all right," she said as she handed him his change.

"Real smooth, lover boy," he cursed himself on the way to his van. His face felt flushed with embarrassment as he saw his reflection in the driver's side mirror. Feeling alone, as only a soldier can feel when away from family and friends, he drove around lost in his thoughts. Not liking crowded places, yet in need of company, he drove out to the mall.

He ordered a cup of coffee and sat in the open dining area to observe people in his line of sight. His frame of mind made him envious of all the couples holding hands and laughing with each other. He couldn't help but admire a man and woman, in their seventies, sitting next to him. They were still together and looked as though they still cared for each other. They were talking quietly to one another in a language developed from years of living together, of growing towards becoming one person, until their identities were completely intertwined. He noticed the eyes of the old woman, how they sparkled when she looked at her husband. True love, he thought.

He was beginning to feel uncomfortably anxious being around so many people. He left the mall and drove slowly back to post. He needed someone he could talk to, someone he could love, someone to love him in return. Although there were times when he was tempted, he had never sought out a prostitute. He could not bring a woman down to that level. He had too much respect for women. He placed all of them in the same category with his mom. No, he could not cheapen his mother's image by such an act. He had slept with his ex-girlfriend, but he had thought they were going to get married.

He found himself pulling into the parking lot of his company headquarters. Too early to sleep, he walked over to the day room. Each company had a room set aside where soldiers could spend their free time. It had a pool table and a TV and maybe even a ping-pong table. A loud voice, gruff and sarcastic by nature, came from the couch placed in front of the TV.

"Stop that fucking racket! I'm trying to watch TV!" The angry voice was directed towards two young specialists who had been shooting pool. Laying down their cue sticks, they quietly left the room. The gruff voice belonged to a stocky man with a bulldog neck and head. His head was completely without hair and cast a small reflection from the overhead lights. He was still in uniform and sat slumped on the couch with a beer in one hand and a cigar in the other. He did not know the guy personally, but he instantly recognized the type of character before him. The man had no leadership ability. He was just a bully who pushed people by fear and intimidation.

Sitting down in a chair he picked up a magazine and leafed through it. Suddenly he became aware that he was being observed. He knew what was coming. "What are you doing here? Don't tell me you're thinking about going SF."

"Starting next week," he said in as disinterested voice as he could.

"YOU! You're too fucking small to be in this man's outfit. I start training at the same time. Bet you won't last the first week!" he said taking a puff on his cigar.

Looking at the man's collar he saw that he was a sergeant first class, which meant he was out ranked by this slob one full grade. Standing up, he placed the magazine down on the table and locked eyes with his tormentor. "No disrespect to your rank, sergeant, but fuck you!" He left the room, knowing the bully would not follow. There was no one else in the room and his kind needed an audience.

He went to his room and laid down on his bunk looking at the ceiling. He wondered if the bull dog's comments were true. Was he biting off more than he could chew? His thoughts shifted to what the first sergeant had said earlier that day about the John Wayne types not being able to hang.

"Well, you've made it this far, don't let some asshole stop you now," he said out loud to himself.

He thought back to his childhood, the bullies he had to contend with every day, their constant remarks about his size. He remembered the day the principal's son started shoving him and saying in a loud voice for everyone to hear, "Look at you! You're poor! You can't even afford clothes to wear. Where did you get those rags? From the city dump?" Each comment was followed by a push. The principal's son, a good head taller than he, should not have pushed him. Eyes showed delight in the attention and encouragement he was receiving from the other kids gathered around the two of them. "Look at the holes in your shirt! Bet all you ever eat is beans, you stupid Indian." Another push. The laughter of the other kids was ringing in his ears.

"Indian trash!" the larger boy sneered with another push.

The bully's sneer turned to surprise when a small fist slammed into his eye. A circle formed quickly around the two of them. The other kids were all shouting encouragement to the principal's son to beat him into a pulp. He got in the better punches. The bigger boy tripped him. He held on though and made the bully fall with him. The two of them began rolling over and over on the ground. Suddenly, he was on top of the bully smashing blow after blow as hard as he could on the hated face before him. He could not see or hear anything else. There was a red fog closing around his eyes that shut out everything but that face. Only fear and pain stared back at him. His arms were tired, but he forced them to pound the blood-stained face again and again.

He felt the rough hands of an adult grabbing him by the hair, pulling him off. His own tears flew from his face as he struggled to get loose to attack his tormenter again. The gradual rush of sounds returned to his head. The fog cleared from his vision. The kids told the teacher he was the one who had started it. His protest was cut short by the rough hands pulling him by his hair to the office. The principal, after hearing what the teacher had to say, made him bend over and struck him with a paddle. The stings from the paddle did not hurt him as much as the words that the principal spoke before striking him that day. "You will never amount to anything. Your kind never does!" The paddle struck him again and again.

The teacher, his teacher, said, "Hit him again. He still isn't crying." He refused to cry for them that day and never cried for anyone since that day. Why had he thought of that? He wondered.

He lit a cigarette and noticed a slight shaking of his hands. He just as quickly put the cigarette out. He got up and changed into shorts and running gear. He was good at running even though he smoked. He could run a mile in less than five minutes. He consistently ran five miles under thirty minutes. His mind seemed to think best when he ran. Tonight his pent-up emotions and uncertainty of the future would take him eight miles. As he sprinted into the company area using up the last of his energy, the first sergeant was standing in the door way of the orderly room smoking a cigarette.

"Airborne," said the first sergeant. "All the way!"

He took a hot shower and went to bed feeling better about himself. His last thought was of the stunning redhead. Wish she were single, he thought, just as sleep overtook him. That night, his mother came to him in his dreams as she often did. Her smile was as beautiful as he remembered, but for some reason there were tears in her eyes. Her dark eyes were sad.

The 0500 hours formation consisted of about forty soldiers standing in one mass rather than platoon-sized elements. The first sergeant called out their names alphabetically from a clipboard. Each man was sounding off with, "Here, first sergeant!" When roll call was completed, the first sergeant announced that all last names beginning A through M were to fall out and form a separate formation. The remaining soldiers were told to fall back into the barracks and clean the rooms and latrines. They were called to attention by the fist sergeant and dismissed to finish getting their personal gear in order and eat breakfast at the small company mess hall. His room was already neat, so he ambled over to the mess hall, smelling the aroma of coffee and bacon fifty feet before entering the door. The ashes of the sweaty cook's cigar threatened to drop any second. He plopped some scrambled eggs on his tray and a scoop of what was supposed to be fried potatoes. He could not figure out how the Army managed to remove all taste and texture from food. Two slices of bacon and a slice of toast completed his breakfast.

Getting a cup of dark, rich coffee, he seated himself at the far corner table in the mess hall. Others were going through the chow line, and the hum of nervous voices soon filled the room. The sergeant first class with the bald head came in, walking with the unmistakable swagger of someone used to getting his way. He deliberately bumped into soldiers standing in line as they tried to move out of his way. He went to the front of the line. The bully shoved his tray under the cook's nose and demanded a double serving. The cook slowly took the cigar from his mouth and dropped the ashes into the sergeant's tray. Then he turned to the soldier behind him and yelled, "Next!" After several soldiers had passed through the line, the sergeant first class slammed his tray on the counter and left.

He found himself in the group of soldiers at the 0700 hours formation. As soon as the others had fallen back into the barracks with the usual pissing and moaning about clean-up details, the first sergeant called each man and gave them a sheet of paper. When his turn came, one glance at the paper told him he would be spending the better part of the day in the Army hospital. He loaded into the back of the waiting two-and-a-half-ton truck, and they were soon on their way.

The truck had not left the company area before the usual GI bragging and bantering had started. "Man, I went to this topless bar last night where you sit in a chair and the girl dances right in front of you!

The girl who served me beer set my beer mug on the bar and squatted right on top of my glass and jiggled her tits in my face."

"Did you get a date with her?" someone asked.

"No," said the center of attention, "I said, 'Sis, when are you coming home?'" Laughter and a few remarks about other sisters and their ability to swim out to troop ships or do squat thrusts on fire hydrants continued until the trucks pulled into the hospital parking lot. He looked at his sheet and confirmed that he was to report to x-ray first. Pictures were taken of his collarbone, and he was sent to the waiting room.

After about an hour of reading outdated *Readers Digest* and *Time* magazines, his name was called out by a heavy-set nurse who escorted him to a small office. Another thirty minutes elapsed as he studied the bone structure chart on the wall. He hated Army hospitals. They were always full of too many patients and never enough doctors. A young doctor came into the small room. He pulled out a set of x-rays and placed them on the wall. He looked at them for a few minutes. He could see with his untrained eye the side that appeared twice as large as the other, where calcium had fused it back together.

"Looks ok to me," said the young doctor. "But with what you're going to be putting it through, it will give you some trouble. I will sign an approval for training. However, should it start causing you too much discomfort, be sure and let a medic know." He assured the doctor he would, but he knew that would be the last thing he would do. With a sigh of relief he took the approval and proceeded to his next station.

The psych unit was his next stop, where once again he waited for over an hour before finally being ushered into another small waiting room. "No couch," he said to no one as he looked around the room.

"Would you like one?" said a voice behind him. Embarrassed for the second time, he turned around to see an older doctor with kind eyes smiling at him. The doctor immediately got down to business as he offered him a seat. After several questions about his personal life, covering what state he was from to if he had any brothers and sisters, the doctor asked him, "Could you kill a three-year-old child?"

The question had taken him by complete surprise. "No, sir!"

"Not under any circumstances?" asked the doctor. Here it is, he thought to himself, If I don't give the response he is looking for, I'm out.

Although he could say what he thought the doctor wanted to hear, he had been briefed to be completely honest with himself.

"Truthfully, no, I could not, not under any circumstances, sir!" The doctor scribbled a few lines on his paper and handed it to him, telling him he was free to go. He dreaded what he might see. He glanced down at the doctor's chicken scratch; he had been approved! He went outside to smoke a cigarette and saw other soldiers from his company getting on the truck. He followed suit. Some would spend the entire day roaming the halls from one clinic to another getting poked, shot, x-rayed, and lost. He and the men on the truck had lucked out. His thoughts were interrupted as the truck whined to life, spewing smoke from the stack, and made a hasty departure from the parking lot.

The usual GI talk and joking picked up as the truck gained speed. "Man! That fuckin' doctor stuck his finger so far up my ass I was choking!"

"Are you sure it was his finger?"

"Dunno and don't care 'cause I passed!" came the response amid laughter.

There were a few men who were quiet. Some of the soldiers were sitting on the wooden troop seats with their heads down. One such individual was sitting beside him. A glance at his paper showed he had flunked the psych interview. When they arrived at the barracks, they turned their papers into the orderly room and went to chow. The soldiers who were not so fortunate were sent to their rooms to pack and relocate to another unit.

The next several days were the same: getting shots and updating their personal records file. A few details, mostly just make-work to keep them busy. Still they were done by four o'clock, and the rest of the day they were left to themselves.

The company slowly filled until by the end of the week they had 190 soldiers. They had completed the in-processing and would depart for Camp McCall the following day. His bags were packed, and his van placed in storage for safekeeping. As he lay on his bunk, day dreaming, the company clerk knocked on his door.

"Sorry to trouble you, sergeant. The first sergeant wants to see you. He said it was important."

The vivid image of his mother's face came to him. Something was wrong at home. He knew it. He had a feeling deep down in his gut. He knocked on the first sergeant's door. The eyes of the first sergeant told him he was correct.

"Sit down, sergeant. I'm afraid I have received some bad news from the American Red Cross. Your father is in the hospital. He's had a heart attack. I'm sorry. I will sign you out on emergency leave. But you understand, the next class for phase one training will not start until January 4th. That means you will be placed in this company as a holdover until then."

Two months of detail, he thought. Without hesitation he said, "I have to go." He would do it for me.

The first sergeant then took out his wallet and gave him a hundred dollars. "Don't argue, just pay me back when you can. Now go get ready. I will have your leave forms typed by the time you turn all your gear into supply.

He ran to his room and stuffed all he owned into his duffel bag. He took his rucksack and other items to supply and assured the supply sergeant he would be back. The supply sergeant, a sergeant first class with whom he had not spoken more than a few brief words, pulled out his wallet and emptied the contents on the table. He ordered him to take the money.

The supply sergeant said, "Don't argue. Just pay me back when you can."

The clerk gave him a ride in the first sergeant's jeep to the holding pen where his van was stored. The clerk said in a quiet voice that he would be praying for his dad. This brought tears to his eyes that he hid from the clerk by checking the oil in the van's engine. He shook hands with the company clerk and then pulled his van onto the road. He headed to his hometown. A long night awaited him as he prepared himself for the twenty-plus hours drive.

He preferred to drive at night: less traffic to worry about. He could allow his mind to wander. A cool breeze coming through the window helped keep him awake. He was worried about his dad, of course. He was the only family he had left. There had been an older sister, but she had died from a ruptured appendix before he was born. His dad could not talk about her very much. He would say sometimes what a free-spirited young girl she had been. He would say she had been a daddy's girl and then stop talking as his lower lip quivered. His dad would always turn away or change the subject. Her third grade picture was placed in a frame that hung on the living room wall. He could remember as a young boy, his father looking at her picture and his mother's picture. They hung side by side, and he would sigh. He could see the pain in his father's face, and his knuckles would turn white as he made a fist. He never interrupted his dad when he came in and saw him looking at their pictures.

His dad was just under six-foot with wavy red hair. An Irishman, he had moved back onto the land in 1935. He walked with a limp from a leg injury. No one knew where he had lived prior to this. He spent a year living by himself and making repairs to the small house. He met and fell in love with his mom. He married her on the Indian reservation. The tribe had adopted him. And the two of them had lived happily and alone until his sister was born the following year. His sister looked exactly like his mother, dark hair and eyes. He resembled his mother with the exception of the green eyes he had inherited from his father. He had spent his entire life on land that bordered an Indian reservation. Almost a thousand acres of rocky hills and steep slopes, unsuitable for raising crops, but excellent for wild game. This property had been in his father's family for several hundred years. His grandparents had lived on this land as their parents had done. There was a family cemetery resting on top of the hill behind the house. His mother and sister were buried there beside his grandparents and his great-grandparents.

His father was a tall, good-looking man with a limited education. Yet he was wise in many ways. He moved away from home in his early teens and worked in the steel mills around Pittsburgh. He sent most of his money home. He returned home when his folks took ill with the flu. After they died, he drifted for a number of years. He hitched rides on the trains and lived a hobo's life as though time and distance could erase his loss.

His dad had taken him to visit his mother's people on the reservation several times when he was growing up. There were no grandparents on his mother's side. They all died from the flu epidemic during World War I. After his mother's death, he had to go with his dad whenever and wherever he went. There was no one to watch him, and he was too young to stay by himself. His dad worked for a farmer from sunup to sundown. He spent a lot of hours in their old pickup truck. The farmer would not allow him to wander around the farm. His wife never invited him into the house, so he spent all of his time in the old truck. Sometimes when the farmer was not looking, his dad would get the newspaper out of the farmer's trash and give it to him. He taught himself to read by the time he was five. He didn't know what all the words meant, but he could pronounce them correctly. His dad would not work for anyone unless they agreed to pay him at the end of the day's work.

"You never know if tomorrow will ever come," his dad would say. "So it's better to take your wages when you earn them." That was how he remembered their life together. Getting up in the pre-dawn hours, eating whatever they had for breakfast, washing his face in a pan of warm water his dad had heated for him on the wood-burning stove.

The old pickup did not have a working heater. In the wintertime he was bundled up in blankets as they made their drive to work. His dad was constantly wiping the fog from the windshield as they drove along the bumpy road. Always the same words of caution from his dad, "Now stay in the truck, son. Stay bundled up. I'll be back in a little bit."

At lunchtime his dad would return. He was allowed to get out of the truck to pee. They would eat a baloney sandwich together, and then he returned to the truck for more hours of waiting until his dad was through working for the day.

As soon as his dad got paid for his day's work they would go to the small country store. They bought what they would need for that evening and the following day: a pack of Camel cigarettes for his dad, baloney for the next day, a pint of milk, a dollar's worth of gas for the truck, and several eggs or a few potatoes. There would be a bottle of soda pop for him and sometimes a candy bar. He never asked for the candy. He would spend his time in the store looking at it until his dad would say, "Get what you want and let's go."

The drive to their home was a slow, bumpy ride down an old logging trail to the house his dad had built. His dad would cook dinner for them on the old wood-burning stove. The house was an icebox, and the two of them would shiver until the fire heated up the room. There was no electricity, so everything had to be done by the kerosene lamp. He would gather twigs and wood chips for a fire in the morning. They would eat dinner together and talk. They would just sit there for several hours with the glow of the kerosene lamp reflecting off their faces. He never tired of listening to his father's stories about the good old days. They would talk about the Bible and politics. Sometimes his dad would tell him about his mother. He would fall asleep in his chair listening to his dad talking about her. The heat from the stove gave warmth to his body. The memories of his mother fed him the necessary fuel for his soul.

The winter months were harsh for them. Snowdrifts would sometimes cover the house almost completely. His dad could not get out for weeks at a time, so they had to eat whatever they had available. Many times he went to sleep with a stomach ache from trying to digest a lard sandwich. He could not use the outhouse on those cold nights, so his dad had fashioned a five-gallon bucket into a makeshift indoor toilet. Dad took a cardboard box and cut a round circle from the bottom of it. It was placed over the can so he could sit without falling in.

Water came from a well behind their house. His dad had dug it by hand and lined it with stones. It would freeze over in the wintertime, and they would have to chip at the ice that formed about a foot thick to get to the water. After that was done, they used a bucket tied to a rope which was lowered and raised by hand. Occasionally, a rabbit or some other animal would find its way into the well, and they would not be able to drink from it for several days. He was not permitted to go near the well until he was much older—although he did climb up on the sides and peek in from time to time when his dad wasn't looking.

The furnishings inside the house were very sparse. The kitchen consisted of a wooden table, two chairs, and the old cook stove. It was the same one his mother had used to made those delicious blackberry pies. He could still smell and taste them.

The living room held a potbelly stove, a wash stand with a pan for bathing, and a couch. His room had an old dresser and a bed. His dad slept on the couch. Next to his room was the room that had the pictures of his mother and sister on the wall with a picture of the Lord's Last Supper above them. It was the room she had died in. They never used this room. The cook stove had been moved to its present location, and the outside door closed off. Sometimes when he missed his mom he would sit in the easy chair and read, placing him near but not too near this dreaded room.

He could feel her presence at times but not always during the day. When her spirit did come to him, he would forget about reading and stare at her picture. He would sit for hours, not saying anything, just feeling her in the room with him. She would come to him at night in his dreams. Her smile was all the encouragement he needed to go to bed to see her.

Many nights he used to cry himself to sleep, worried sick about losing his dad. What would happen to him? Where would he live? Would he live in an orphanage? Who would take care of him? Or would some nice couple adopt him and buy him new clothes to wear. These thoughts would make him feel guilty, and he would pray to God not to take his daddy.

He was about halfway home and getting tired. He was not hungry, but knew he should eat. Pulling into a truck stop he ordered a sandwich and a cup of coffee. After a few stretches and some fast exercises, he was back on the road. He passed a long-haired hippie wearing dirty jeans with holes in the knees. He thought about giving him a ride for the company but decided not to. He felt like being alone with his thoughts.

One thing his dad lacked was the culinary skills of a good cook. His belly used to rumble all the time from the potatoes fried in huge amounts of lard. Just before they could turn a golden brown the way he liked them, his dad would pour water over them. "Stewed tatters" his dad called them, served them in a bowl with grease floating on top. They would eat the potatoes and then sop up the excess liquid with bread. No wonder his stomach was always upset. Just thinking about the meals they shared together sent a shudder through him. They didn't have fresh vegetables or fruit often.

One day as he was sitting in the old pickup truck reading, his dad came in from work early. He looked upset. The farmer he had worked for had told him he was cutting his wages from a dollar an hour to seventy-five cents. His dad quit. What would they do now? After two weeks of looking, his dad found employment with another farmer. This farm was twenty miles on the other side of the mountain, and it would take the two of them over three hours to drive it. The problem was solved as the new employer had an old two-story farm house the two of them could live in. He gave it to them rent free, and they could check on their old house anytime. For the first time in his life he had an indoor toilet and electricity. But that only lasted until the first electric bill arrived and they couldn't pay the bill. It was promptly shut off, and they were back to the old kerosene lamp.

The move coincided with his first year of school. He entered first grade with enthusiasm. He quickly realized that kids are, by nature, cruel. His first day kids laughed at him for his ragged clothes. As the days turned into months, he was forced to fight again and again. The kids made fun of him for being a poor Indian. His teacher had nothing but contempt in her eyes whenever she looked upon him. They were not his mother's eyes. He took daily beatings. He never told his dad about what the fights were over, although occasionally a note would be sent home with him. He never gave these to his dad.

There was a barn beside the house they lived in with ropes and pulleys. He would swing from one side to the other. He fell and landed safely on the bales of hay beneath him. There were woods across the dirt road to explore, with animals to watch. In the forest he could be anything he wanted to be. Some days he was space man in a space ship flying through the dark unknown to rescue a planet. Happening across a bent tree sent his imagination soaring. He turned into a cowboy breaking rough and wild horses. He could read the small animal trails and became an Indian searching for signs of the enemy.

The hay was removed from the barn during the winter months to feed the cattle. It was around the same time that the rats migrated into the house. One night as he lay sleeping, a huge rat crawled up the side of his bed and began gnawing on his hand. He didn't feel anything at first, just an odd pressure. The rat's teeth grated against his bone. Suddenly his hand awoke to the sensation, and he jumped from the bed. The rat fled back into its hole frightened. His dad made him a bandage from an old sheet and soaked his hand in turpentine. His dad worried about the rat attack for over a month. The next time his dad got paid, he went without the cigarettes and bought rat poison. There were many times his dad would fix him dinner and not eat.

"I'm not hungry, son," he would say in an offhanded way like he didn't have a care in the world. His dad would even pack his lunch for school using the leftovers. He suddenly realized how many sacrifices his dad had made for him over the years. He was proud of his life. He was proud of his Indian heritage, but most of all he was proud of his father. The hardships that the two of them endured only now seemed like hardships, after years of reflection and compared to his current lifestyle. He was grateful and considered himself very fortunate to have shared such challenges with a good man. Who did he take after? He could see the resemblance of his mother in his face. But where did his intellect come from? He was a good engineer in the Army. He could solve complex mathematical problems in his head. He had developed a photographic memory somewhere along the way. He could instantly recall any book he had ever read. He had loved to read. He even taught himself to speed read up to a thousand words a minute, with a mere glance at any paper, its contents were digested instantly. Since he joined the Army he had gradually found that the same quick reading was possible with people. An instant after introductions, he could read the character of the person before him, not unlike a first impression. It was a gift. It told him if the person before him could be trusted in combat or in life.

After eighteen hours of straight driving and breaking all speed limits, he arrived in his hometown. Bittersweet memories flooded his senses as he passed the school. He arrived at the hospital and asked for his dad's room number. He entered just as a nurse was leaning over him, adjusting the sheets and pillow. She glanced up and smiled. "You must be the guy he keeps talking about. He's doing fine. He's had a good night's rest. If you need me just page me on this." She explained the operation of the remote call button and left them alone.

His dad looked a lot older to him, more than he had anticipated. He was used to coming home on leave over the years and could never adjust to the mild shock that always went through him. His aged appearance was magnified by the distance between them.

His father's hands were calloused and scarred from years of hard work, the deep lines around his eyes from squinting at the sun and wind. Deep furrows of worry and depression lay across his forehead. He was almost completely bald with the exception of a thin line running around the top of his ears. His arms, once muscular and strong, lay in a soft mass of flabby tissue.

His father stirred in his sleep. The lines on the monitor jumped in a frantic disarray. He took his dad's hands in his. His dad opened his eyes and looked at him. "Hello, boar head," his dad said to him in a raspy voice.

"Hello, pops," he replied. "The things you do to get attention."

"When did you get here?"

"About five minutes before you woke up," he said. "You just rest; I'm not going anywhere." His dad drifted back to sleep. He leaned over and said in a quivering whisper, "I love you dad." His dad's hand gripped his tighter, and he knew his dad had heard him. He stayed there for the rest of the day and all through the night. He remained bent over the bed, his elbows rested on the mattress, holding the coarse and calloused hands of his father. His eyes were fixed on the monitor. It made an unsteady rhythm that mimicked his father's weak heart. He never took his eyes off the monitor. Maybe if he used enough will power, he could give him strength. He caressed the familiar hands with his fingers. He felt a closeness that was uncommon among most men. His thoughts drifted over the past. These thoughts consumed him, and he was lifted off into a state of blankness. He didn't feel any pain or stiffness even though he was in an awkward position. He just sat there, emembering.

After three years of living away from home, they made a weekend visit to their little house. They cleaned it and spent the night there. The next morning as they were about to leave, his dad's former employer pulled into the driveway. His shiny new car made their old pickup truck look even more dilapidated and gloomy.

"Just thought I'd drop by and see how you were doing," he said. "Been by a few times but could never catch you at home. Would you be willing to come back to work for me if I paid you a dollar and twenty-five cents an hour?"

They moved the following day. They were both happy to be home. They placed his mother's and sister's pictures back on the wall and quietly left the room.

His only regret was going to the old school on the reservation. He knew the same unlikable kids would be there waiting for him. It would be the same. He'd be alienated and ostracized. Only this time, because of the white blood that flowed in his veins. The teacher at the white school made fun of his beliefs. She would often ask him a question and laugh with the class when he gave an answer to where his people came from.

"The ground," he would reply.

And she would squint at him and ask him, yet, another cruel question. "How many worlds have there been before this one?"

"Three. This is the fourth and last world, my mother told me." He thought that because his mother had taught him this, they would respect his beliefs. Instead they had all laughed at him. Some of the bigger boys beat him at recess and tried to make him change his mind. He would not, particularly because it was one of the few things he retained of his mother's. He could still see the teacher smiling as they took turns hitting him.

He would be in fourth grade when school opened in a month. He spent that time begging his dad to allow him to stay home rather than sitting in the old truck all day. His dad finally relented, and he spent the following weeks exploring the woods and creeks around the house. He taught himself to read the tracks of different animals and soon began experimenting with snares. He became proficient at catching small animals, mostly squirrels and rabbits. Their diet improved over the coming years as his hunting skills improved. He eventually learned to tan the hides of the animals with his dad's help. In the summer he roamed the hills and mountains; he learned how to live in the forest. He was happiest during these long days. The forest taught him many things. There were spirits that whispered to him. They were around him day and night, and he learned to have no fear. As he became older, he knew these were the spirits of his ancestors and they were watching over him.

The years passed more rapidly. By the time he was in eighth grade, he had grown as tall as he would ever be. He was making money trapping animals for their furs. He sold them at the old country store. The kids quit making fun of him. After a few of them received a broken nose or lost a tooth, word soon got around not to mess with the half-Indian kid.

When he turned sixteen, he wanted to quit school and find a job. His dad sat him down and had a long talk with him. "Son, your mother wanted you to get an education. She did not want you to be forced to work like I still have to just to make ends meet. So I'm not asking you, I'm telling you to fulfill your mom's wishes."

What could he do? He had to graduate. He now went about his chores and school work with a new found enthusiasm. He would cut enough fire wood for the evening meal and breakfast. He drew water from the well and washed and hung his clothes so they would dry in time for school. He put on his buckskin shirt, pants, and moccasins, and departed for the woods. He checked on his traps and snares with the bow and quivers he and his dad had made together over the long winter months. He would get home by the time his dad arrived back from work. When he finally did get home, his dad started a fire for the evening meal. He would skin and clean whatever he had captured. After doing his homework by kerosene lamp, the two of them would talk for a few hours before going to bed. Each night his mother would come to him in his dreams, smiling and expressing her pride and joy in her little warrior. Because of her nightly visits, he never suffered the nightmare of her death. He knew she was still there with him.

A slight moan interrupted his thoughts, pulling him back to the present. His dad coughed and tried to move his arms. The exertion was more than he had strength for. The brief distraction from his thoughts brought to the forefront of his mind the pain that was coursing up his legs and back. He shifted his weight and adjusted his body position to relieve the stress. "Take it easy, pops, I'm here with you. Just take it easy. When we get you out of here, you're going to come live with me." If his dad would not move, then he would get out of the Army and come home to take care of him. The first hours of daylight filtered through the east window. He had been interrupted several times by the night staff as they checked on his dad. The nurse who had greeted him the day before came into the room with the energy of someone who had a good night's sleep.

"I heard you haven't moved from that spot all night. Why don't you go to the cafeteria and get something to eat? He will be fine until you get back." Prying his fingers gently from his dad's, he looked around to ensure no one was looking. He gave his dad a kiss on the cheek and tiptoed out of the room. He ate a quick breakfast of scrambled eggs and potatoes, washing everything down with several cups of coffee. He took a cup with him and stood outside enjoying the crisp morning air and a cigarette. Suddenly, an electric shock went through him. A slight bell sound, like the twinkling of a very faint light, ricocheted in his ears. There was a distinct presence around him which faded rapidly. He threw his cigarette down and took the stairs three at a time to the third floor. As he entered the room, he knew he was too late. A doctor and several nurses were working on what he knew was just a corpse. The nurse, who had told him to go eat, intercepted him with tears in her eyes.

"I am so . . ." The words curdled in her throat. "I am so very sorry."

He nodded and went into the room just as the doctor was leaving. He walked up to the bed and took his dad's hand one last time. He said in a voice beyond grief and despair, "Thanks for being my friend."

He buried his dad next to his mother and sister in the small cemetery plot. His dad had kept the grave site clean for all those years. There were wildflowers and a single rose bush at the head of each grave. His mother had loved the sweet perfumed smell of wild pink roses. The small wooden fence which surrounded the plot was its sentry and protector. The driver of the hearse stood off to the side for a few minutes before getting into the car. He drove slowly down the rut-filled road like his father used to do. There was no one else to share his grief. He stood there for several hours pouring out his heart until he had said all that his heart had to say. He walked, taking careful steps, to the house his dad had refused to leave. He was thankful that his father had managed to get electricity and indoor pluming installed on his meager military pay. He sent money home every month to pay for the electric bill and enough for his dad to live on. And the money he received for re-enlisting for six years had bought his father a new pickup truck.

He looked around the room where he and his dad had spent so much time together. On the wall was pinned a heart he had made for Valentine's Day when he was in third grade—a somewhat misshapen red heart with a white lace piece of paper in the center cut in the shape of a heart. Something a child would give to his mother, yet something his dad had kept all these years. He felt truly alone for the first time in his life. His heart would never heal. All he knew and loved ended up wiped away. He began to take down the pictures of his mother and sister. He placed them on the floor and gathered the cabin's contents into one large heap in the center of the room. He spent the night in his childhood home reliving some of the memories. And somewhere amidst his remembering, he fell asleep. His mother did not come to him.

He awoke the next morning with a start. Daylight filtered through the dirty window. He got up and poured kerosene on the floor. He let it soak for a few minutes. He made a trail out the front door through the yard. He glanced back one more time and set a match to it. A muffled whumpf could be heard as he headed to his van. He knew he would never return to this place once so full of happiness. At least not in this life.

He did not report in on his first day arriving back to Fort Bragg. He felt the urge to be around people without a military lifestyle. He stopped at a bar in downtown Fayetteville and ordered a beer. He sat in the corner and listened to the off-duty soldiers repeat the same lines to the same type of girls he had heard before. Changing his mind, he left his beer untouched and drove slowly around town until he got hungry. He had not had anything to eat since he left home. He would have a steak to celebrate his father's memory and a glass of wine to toast his one and only friend. The thought seemed to make him feel a little better. He went to a small, uncrowded restaurant. After being seated he enjoyed a cup of good coffee and a cigarette. A young girl came in and was seated at a table next to his. He recognized her instantly. She was the pretty redhead that worked in the PX. He could feel his face turning red as he recalled his unsuccessful attempt to ask her for a date. Seeing that she was by herself, he said loud enough for her to hear,

"I thought you said you were married?" She looked up from her menu at him, and he was surprised again as he found recognition float through her eyes.

"I say that to everyone," she said. "It keeps my line moving and my job secure. Have you found anyone to show you around?" The comment brought a sudden rush of blood to his cheeks. For a few seconds they sat in awkward silence until he mustered up the only thing he could think to say.

"I thought maybe I should wait until I grow taller." She laughed and the ice was broken.

"May I join you?" She nodded her head, and he moved to her table.

The waitress appeared amused.

"So, are you really single? Tell me more about yourself." She cocked her head to one side and smiled, "Yes I'm really single. I was an Army brat. I moved from post to post and country to country all my life. My dad is about to retire. They just bought a house on the outskirts of Fayetteville. Ummm. . . I work full time, and I'm going to school part time. I'm going to be a nurse. I'll be done in another year. What about you?"

He told her what he was doing at Fort Bragg. They compared each other's interest in food and recreation. He was surprised to hear she enjoyed camping and hiking through the mountains. He could sense that she was as lonely as he was. He asked her if they could take in a movie. Leaving her car in the restaurant parking lot, they drove to the mall in his van. As he drove through the busy traffic, she continued talking about her life. She was an only child, admittedly spoiled. She had been to nine different schools before graduating in Heidelberg, Germany. She had moved back to the states with her parents and still lived with them. He told her of his dad's untimely death, and he saw a sincere sympathy in her eyes. There was a moment of silence as he regained his inner composure. He went on to explain how this had placed him in a hold-over company for the next few months. He would be doing top secret missions on post—such as raking leaves and picking up pine cones.

"But you're a sergeant. You won't have to actually do the work yourself." He thought about telling her that he saw sergeant majors in Special Forces doing the same details. But he did not want her to think he was pulling her leg. They could not find a movie they wished to see. They both secretly wanted to spend time together and share in each other's world. They drove around until he stopped at an all-night restaurant, and they drank coffee and talked. He did not realize how late it was until the drunks started coming in from the closing bars. The noise consumed their conversation. It was impossible to even think in your head it was so loud. He realized how late it was, so he drove her back to her car. She gave him her phone number and the best times to call. He thanked her and said he would call. He wanted to kiss her but couldn't find the courage to do it. He drove to a motel and spent the night sleeping soundly, better than he had in years. Perhaps he had found someone after all. She was everything he was looking for. He just hoped that he had what she wanted. He thought of her sweet smile before he drifted to sleep. It lit up her face and sparkled through her eyes. There was goodness there. Her smile was like his mother's, and he knew, once again, he was someone special. His mother appeared in his dreams that night; she was smiling. He awoke at 0900 hours. He had not slept that long in years. He got out of bed and quickly did the three S's. After dressing in his fatigues and boots, he ate breakfast before heading back on post to sign in. He stopped at finance and drew his pay for the month. The first thing he did after signing back on duty was to repay the first sergeant and the supply sergeant. Raking the fall leaves and picking up pine cones—the life of a true soldier, he thought. There were six other soldiers being held over with him. Each morning they would report to the orderly room and receive instructions on what area of the post was in need of their expertise. They would load onto the back of a truck with bags and rakes to make a full frontal assault on the area. He had the pleasure of seeing the sergeant first class he had words with in the day room return, given his walking papers. He looked worn and haggard as he drove off the compound. He stood with his rake in his hand and waved goodbye to him. A whole month of hard labor, and they had the enemy in full retreat. Or at least they thought they did until a storm with forty-mile-an-hour winds came through, and the area looked as though it had never been touched.

He spent his weekends with her. He had taken her to the drop zone a few times whenever there was a fun jump he could get on. She watched him land his parachute within fifty feet of her one day and saw him get his ass chewed out by the drop zone safety officer for doing it. She mimicked the officer's voice from time to time. She did this to watch his face turn red. Her laughter was like music, he thought. He would have done anything to hear her laugh. The time passed all too quickly. He spent Thanksgiving and Christmas at her house. Her parents seemed to accept him. They would have preferred a doctor, he thought, still they did their best to make him feel welcome.

As they sat around the Christmas tree, each taking a turn unwrapping their presents, a flashback to a sad yet happy time came to the forefront of his mind. It was two years after his mother's death when he asked his dad if they could put up a Christmas tree. He remembered the painful look of despair that crossed his father's face. He was too young to understand that his father was still in mourning for the loss of his wife.

"Sure, son. We can do that." Together the two of them hiked through the mountain on a cold December morning to locate the perfect tree. He insisted on cutting it down as his father stood by and watched. It took the two of them to drag the tree back to their cabin. His dad set the tree up in a stand while he searched for his mother's Christmas tree decorations.

His father told him to go ahead and fix the tree up, and he made an excuse to leave the room. "I better go chop some wood, son. It looks like a cold spell is headed this way." A cold breeze filled the house as his father opened and closed the door behind him. He sat alone with his thoughts of him and his mother decorating the tree together in a far away time and place. He picked up her favorite bulb. It was a brilliant blue with a family sleigh scene painted on it. The people in the sleigh were all waving and smiling. He ran his fingers over it and held the bulb. He enjoyed her memory. His little heart was heavy as he placed the bulb on a branch that was eye level with him. He did not place any thing else on the tree. He put the rest of the decorations back in the box and put them back where they had been stored. He spent the rest of the afternoon looking at the tree and thinking of his mother.

On Christmas Eve he went to bed thinking Santa Claus would stop during the night and leave him some presents. He dreamed of his mother and saw her eyes were happy. He awoke the next morning and hurried from his bed across the cold floor to stare at the tree. There was nothing under it. It was just as he left it the night before. His heart sank as he knew Santa Claus had passed him by. He tried to think of how bad he had been throughout the year, and nothing came to mind.

Later that day, he drove with his father to the farmer's house. They had Christmas dinner there. He had never seen so much food on the table at one time in his life. Even more disturbing was the amount of boundless toys thrown about the living room. The farmer's kids showed him all the things Santa had brought them. When he started to pick up a toy, it was snatched out of his hand.

"That's mine!" the boy yelled and told him never to touch his stuff again.

On the long drive home he said, "Dad, how come that boy got all those toys from Santa, and I didn't get anything?"

There was a long pause as his father swallowed several times. "I guess Santa just forgot where you lived, son." They drove in silence the remainder of ride home. As his dad built a fire in the pot belly stove, he stood looking at the tree. After the house warmed up, he took the bulb and placed it back in the box. Without saying anything to his dad, he dragged the tree outside and left it near the wood pile. He awoke sometime in the late night and thought he heard his dad crying. He went back to sleep knowing he was just dreaming. As his dad never cried.

His thoughts were broken as he was nudged in the ribs and heard her say, "Hey! It's your turn. Aren't you going to open your present?"

January 4, 1971

The time had come for him to depart for phase one training. They spent their last free night together eating at the restaurant where they first met. He took her home and kissed her.

"I'll see you in a month if this all goes well." She started to cry. She wanted desperately to tell him not to go, to give up this idea so that they could be together, but she knew he would not do this. Not even for her. She watched him from her door as he walked to his van.

"You know I'm in love with you," she said to his back, loud enough for him to hear.

"Sure hope so," he replied without turning around, "Cause I've been in love with you since I first saw you." Wish my dad could have met her, he thought to himself as he started his van. He inhaled the lingering smell of her perfume and held her in his thoughts as he drove back to his barracks.

Every cloud has a silver lining. Being held back had its advantages. He took the time and studied various details that enabled him to pick up bits and pieces of what he was in for. The soldiers that were returning for medical reasons were the ones he asked questions. He tried to find out as much as possible about how to prepare for his first phase of training.

By the time he was loaded onto the cattle car for the one hour ride, he had a fair idea of what he was getting into. He heard there was no harassment; you could quit at anytime. Day or night, transportation was there for a ride back to Fort Bragg. You did a tremendous amount of running with a sixty-pound rucksack on your back through sand on warm days. The weight of the pack pushed you down in the sand and covered your boots and tripped you on the frozen ridges on cold morning runs. He also learned that any instructor could drop you from the course at any time. He knew he was in for a lot more than what he was being told. Of the nearly 200-man company that departed the day he left on emergency leave, over half had returned in the first two weeks. His stomach lurched when he saw the sergeant first class he had words with in the day room return after two weeks, looking hollow eyed and defeated. He waved goodbye to him with a big smile on his face. He was glad to see his type washed out.

The cattle cars brought them into the gate of Camp McCall. He was mildly impressed with the size of the camp. It could not have covered more than five acres. The troop barracks were a row of small wooden huts and a small building that served as the mess hall. There was a classroom and an orderly room distinguished by the flagpole standing in front. It was not what he had expected. The barracks were made of plywood and sat on a concrete floor with a single light bulb resting in the center of the ceiling. The bunks were made out of an outdated metal that had been discarded by the Army years ago. There was no mattress; in its place was a sheet of plywood bolted to the bed frame. He unrolled his sleeping bag on the bunk and placed his rucksack and duffel bag at the foot of the bed. The latrine and shower was about a hundred feet from his barracks. The shower was a water tank mounted on telephone poles; it contained 500 gallons of cold water. Spartan by any standards, he knew he would have to adjust quickly.

He fell into formation, and they marched the short distance to the classroom. They filed inside and sat down on the wooden benches. A solid wooden plank made of two by sixes served as a table. After they were seated, a sergeant first class entered, and after jumped onto the stage at the front of the classroom, he introduced himself as their TAC sergeant. A few men breathed a sigh of relief. This guy could not have been more than five feet two inches in height.

"Hope he is the one we get to run with," someone behind him whispered.

"Hope he is not the one to run us," he murmured to himself. Tall people were always underestimating short people.

The TAC sergeant gave them a rundown on what they could expect in the following month. He talked about formation times and the uniform to be worn for each one. He finished by saying in a sincere tone, "You have made it this far, and you can make it through this month. There is only one thing that can stop you." Pointing to his head he said,

"It's all up here. Either you want it or you don't. Just remember Amos and Andy will be glad to have you if you quit." Amos and Andy was a term for the 82nd Airborne Division located at Fort Bragg. Amos and Andy referred to the double A on the shoulder patch of the 82nd which meant All-American.

After the initial briefing they started their classes. They worked until dinner time and walked through a building just big enough to hold the canisters of hot chow and food servers. They ate outside on picnic tables. In less than thirty minutes they were rushed back into the classroom where classes continued for another four hours. It started snowing when they were released. Phase one had begun.

0430 hours he was awakened by a tape player coming over the loud speaker. "The Ballad of the Green Berets" blared through the tiny barracks. He got out of his sleeping bag and estimated that the temperature was twenty-five degrees. He pulled on his pants and laced his boots. Outide he fell into a formation with just a T-shirt and rucksack as instructed the day before. He made sure his rucksack weighed at least sixty pounds before going to bed. Now his rucksack was weighed on a scale. He stood there shivering. After all the rucks had been weighed, the short TAC had the first squad leader pick a man from his squad. The TAC sergeant relieved this man of his rucksack and placed it on his back. They were called to attention, and the flag ran up the pole. They stood shaking in the predawn hours as they saluted. Immediately as the last note of reveille drifted away on the loud speaker, order arms and right face was given.

"Double time, march!" And they were off on a brisk run. The small TAC sergeant was in the front leading the formation of slightly more than a hundred men. The run started off as a slow shuffle, then quickened after the first mile. He struggled to adjust the shoulder straps as the pain from the weight and exertion crept into his body. The sand was impossible to give him any friction for running. His feet slipped and slid with each step he took. His breathing became raspy. His lungs frantically searched for more air, and his legs felt the strain of the rucksack and the sand. I can't keep this up much longer, he thought. This is hopeless. He started to fall back when the speed picked up again! How can that little bastard run so fast? The pain became so intense he could not take another step.

After three miles they came within sight of the compound. He could see the lights flickering in the barracks as they rounded a corner of the sandy road. They were nearing the gate when the TAC sergeant took them on a trail that veered left and away from the camp. They increased their pace once again. He was in a fog. Never in his life had he had to run with so much weight so fast for such a distance. After another mile the compound came into view again. This time they entered the gate at a full all out run. Somehow he managed to draw the reserves from his screaming mules and finish with the formation. Quick time march was given, and every man almost stopped in his tracks. Thirty seconds were counted off, and the gate to the compound was closed. Any one outside the compound would have to do a rucksack run after the day's training.

They were dismissed and went back to their barracks. It was all he could do to walk the hundred yards to his bunk and take off his rucksack. He dried himself off with a towel and put on a new T-shirt. He forced himself to eat breakfast which, by now, was served. After gulping a quick meal of scrambled eggs and cold dried potatoes, he doubled time back to his hut. He shaved in the shower room and, like the rest of the men, gave the thought of a cold shower very little consideration. He quickly changed into dry clothing and hung his wet sweat-filled fatigues on a nail by his bunk. He knew they would freeze before they dried. Feeling a little warmer in his fatigues jacket, he went outside to await the next formation just minutes away. He smoked a cigarette with several others. They were all lost in their thoughts, all wondering if it got any worse than this. Four weeks to go. If the runs don't get any worse than this morning and I don't have any unexpected injuries, I think this is going to be a breeze. He was wrong on both counts.

CHAPTER 6

General Patton's speech was on the loud speaker system. It was freezing outside. The warmth of the sleeping bag did little to stop his shivering now that he was fully awake. It was still dark outside. He estimated the time to be about 0430 hours. He had not been to bed before midnight since his arrival. He did not want to get up. The sleeping bag was almost warm. He knew the temperature had dropped to the low teens during the night. And all of them had been issued summer sleeping bags made for warm weather above forty degrees. Every muscle and bone in his body ached from the physical demands placed on them during the past two weeks. He thought about just staying in his sleeping bag until the sun came up and getting a ride back to Fort Bragg. To hell with it. Then he remembered the sergeant first class he saw coming back about this same time when he was on holdover duty.

Patton's speech filled his mind with the men at the Battle of the Bulge. They had to survive in worse conditions than this, being shot at, going without food, and dying from the cold. A feeling of shame came over him. There were no bullets flying around him; no shells bursting over him. How could he think of quitting? Unzipping the sleeping bag he hastily got dressed.

"Be damned if I will be compared to his kind," he said to himself, thinking about the sergeant in the day room once again. He went from bunk to bunk and shook each of the men gently and told them to get up. Three men stayed in their bags, refusing to go through just one more day of the dreaded rucksack run. He tried talking to them, but the three men refused to move. The rest of the men stood around the bunks trying to motivate the three with pleas and threats. It was to no avail as they told everyone to fuck off. They were through. He placed his rucksack on the bed and sat down with his back to it. He gently placed his arms through the shoulder straps and gritted his teeth. He stood up, and wave after wave of pain filled his body. Both of his shoulders were black and bruised. The right one was more painful because of his collarbone, and the break long ago took the weight of the shoulder strap directly. Sometimes during the morning runs he could feel the bone tearing its way through tissue as the rucksack bounced up and down with each step.

Like everyone else in the small shack, his back was now covered with raw scabs. The constant up and down friction of the rucksack each morning had caused them. The scabs did not have time to heal completely and the thin T-shirt did not offer any padding or protection. He knew the scabs would come off as they did every morning. His T-shirt would be soaked with blood from the shoulder blades down to his waist. His thoughts were full of dread when he visualized the morning run. The sixty-pound rucksack rubbed against his back; his scabs tore loose; the blood flowed down his back and mixed with his sweat. Everyday they ran the four miles or more, and everyday someone would refuse to get up. They were down to less than half of the men who had been with him just two short weeks ago. He had taken one shower in the past two weeks. The water was so cold he could not stand under it. He jumped in, got wet, stood shivering as he rubbed himself down with soap and, gasping for breath, rinsed off not knowing or caring if he got all the soap off. The flag went up the pole briskly as they stood at attention.

"Right face!" The now diminished numbers sent a small groan through the formation. "Forward march! Double time march!" The rapid commands came from the TAC sergeant, and the fast seven-minute mile pace had begun. They ran towards the airfield located about two miles from camp. They ran over the frozen sand. The deep ruts were a hazard and caused several men to twist their ankles. Their cries of anguish and despair filled his ears and sent a wave of panic through him.

Several men in front of him tripped on the uneven ground and fell. They suffered later from cuts and bruises on their hands and knees, but the formation hurriedly passed around them. He had fallen several times in the past several days. The open scrapes became a constant reminder to concentrate on his running. They reached the airfield and ran along the full length of it. They were going to circumvent the entire airfield! He expected that today's run would be more than eight miles. The shoulder straps had cut the supply of blood to his arms and sent a tingling sensation through his hands. He bit his bottom lip. The scabs pulled away from his back. Salty sweat merged with a fresh supply of blood and began dripping freely down his backside. The pace had quickened to about a six-minute mile pace. The formation was strung out over a quarter of a mile.

He kept his eyes on the ground directly in front of him and willed his body to pull itself forward a yard at a time. After completing the run around the airfield, they headed back to camp. He forced his mind to shut down, to ignore the pain, the lack of air in his lungs. His single thought was to keep running. He had to finish one more run. He had gone through his reserve strength several miles back. All that he had left was sheer determination. The thought of falling out wasn't possible; the thought of quitting wasn't possible. He visualized the sergeant first class again, how he had so happily smiled and waved goodbye to what he considered a peace of shit just a short time ago. He would not be like him. He would run until his heart gave out, but he would not quit. He wanted to kick the TAC sergeant's ass. The little bastard was chewing a wad of tobacco as if this were a casual morning stroll.

The gates of the camp came into view. He was afraid it would be another mind game, another torturous run veering off on another route for additional one to two miles. Were they going to do this today? He was not sure he could keep the pace to make it to the gate. Would he be forced to fall out? His head was swimming. His eyes had formed a tunnel from looking directly at the ground so long. Dark spots were dancing before his eyes. Somehow he willed his legs to get to the next step, to move forward several more feet. He should hold his head up and be prepared should someone in front of him fall. However, he knew if he took his eyes off the ground he would fall out. The gate was there, and they ran through it, increasing the speed to a full 100-yard dash to the flagpole. He stood in a trance. He did not hear the command to fall out. He saw bodies moving slowly past him to the billets. He stumbled after them in a daze. He sat down on his bunk to remove his rucksack and passed out.

The sweat-soaked T-shirt quickly turned to a cold miserable cloak that surrounded his frame and sapped the heat from his body. His hair, completely wet, had became a strand of ice. The chill gradually brought him back to his surroundings. He was shivering so violently that his eyes had difficulty focusing. Little did he know that he was suffering from hypothermia. Others in the room were in the same state. Several were on the floor where they had fallen. They were shaking, and the cold concrete floor sapped what little heat they had left. He pulled off his shoulder straps and eased himself out of his ruck. He tried to stand up, but his legs refused to move. He bent over and pulled his legs out straight to sit back. The cold caused him to shiver so badly that his fingers were unresponsive. He forced his legs to move. Slowly he got to his feet. His leg muscles felt as though they were made of jelly. He found it difficult to maintain his balance. He walked like a cripple bent over at the waist. His hands used the bunk for support, and he made his way to his duffel bag. He pulled out a set of dry clothing, and he took off his now ice-stiffened T-shirt. He felt the T-shirt rip away a couple scabs from his back.

The pain was heightened by the warm blood that flowed freely. He put on a fresh pair of pants and then tried to lace his boots. His fingers felt as stiff as branch twigs. It was something so simple. Getting dressed was part of his daily routine and yet it was nearly impossible with his shaking fingers. To his dismay, he heard the call for formation over the loud speaker. They had missed breakfast. As quickly as he could, he finished getting dressed. The three men who had stayed in their sleeping bags earlier that morning came in from eating chow. The look on their faces told him everything. They were ashamed. All their hard work was for nothing. He knew that they wished they could take it back. The three of them couldn't look him in the eye as they offered to clean up the billets for the rest of them. They were good soldiers.

The day passed in a blur. He was not sure if he was conscious through most of the classes. On the plus side though, up next was survival training. For the next three days, there would be no food but what they could find and, more importantly, there would be no rucksack runs. He had not slept soundly for the past two weeks. The moans coming from soldiers when they shifted and rolled over on their hard plywood bed kept waking him up. Not only that, but he could not imagine his bones ever getting the cold out of them. They ached, and he laid shivering and moaning like the rest of the men in the small hooch. He dozed fitfully again that night, as he did every night, and dreamed of the two of them sweating on a beach under a blazing hot sun. They had nothing else to do except listen to the ocean's waves under a clear starlit night.

He boiled water in a tin can and added pine needles. He drank it down fast. The warm water held off hypothermia, and the pine needles were a good source of vitamin C. There is not much to eat in the wintertime in North Carolina. They spent the first day building improvised shelters. They spent the second day kicking over old logs looking for grub worms. They proved to be very tasty if cooked over a fire. A live goat was brought in that evening, and the TAC taught a class on how to butcher and skin animals. Each man received a piece of the goat. Some of them boiled the meat with roots, and others roasted theirs over the fire.

He dreaded the return to camp because, for the first time in two weeks, he was warm. The makeshift shelters and small fires in the evening offered a surprising amount of comfort. A large meal awaited them when they walked into camp after three days of mostly pine needle tea. Scrambled eggs were piled high on each man's tray along with scoops of fried potatoes smothered in GI gravy. He took a canteen cup full of hot coffee with him, and he sat on one of the picnic tables. It had snowed during the night. There was about three inches on the ground. And even though it was cold, it seemed like heaven. A sergeant from Texas sat across from him. He shivered uncontrollably. He had voiced his dislike of cold weather numerous times.

"God, I sure do miss Texas," he said as he sat down on the bench. He sneezed, blowing snot and mucus over the tray of food he still held in his hands. The look on his face was one of pure frustration. "Just kill me," the Texan said. He could sympathize, but that didn't stop him from falling off the bench because he was laughing so hard. He could hardly catch his breath. The poor Texan looked at him in bewilderment. Why, in his moment of misery, did everyone just happen to find the humor in it?

They had made it through phase one training. The last week was spent in the swamps around Camp McCall. They walked through the swamps for four to five hours each night before completing a mission on dry land. Then they practiced attacking bridges and placing charges on them; setting up ambushes; sitting frozen for several hours waiting for a patrol to pass by them. The cycle continued. Soon they were in the swamps, wading through freezing water up to their chests. Their arms grew tired because they had to hold their rifles above their heads to keep them from getting wet. The point man had the most difficult job. He would have to break through the thin layer of ice that formed on top of the swamp water. They would walk until daylight, at which time they would establish a base camp on dry land. They could not build a fire and dry themselves out. The smoke would give away their positions. They would eat a little and get as much sleep as they could. They crawled inside their sleeping bags with cold, saturated clothing. During the day they went out on short range patrols. They repeated this process, day after day and night after night, for seven straight days.

Each man averaged two hours of sleep a night, one meal of rations per day. Soon it began to take its toll on all of them. They were haggard and dirty, unshaven and red-eyed, irritable and tired. He dreaded the walks through the swamps as much as the rest of the men. The initial shock of entering the freezing water was almost as bad as the slow numbing cold inching up his legs to his balls and creeping up past the waist. What had been the most difficult phase of training? The rucksack runs were up there; the confidence course they ran through twice a day equaled in pain; but the hardest part of training for him had been the constant reminder that they were not forced to be here. They endured many hardships. The weak and timid had been weaned out. Of the hundred men that started out three short weeks ago, there remained forty-two. One advantage to winter in the swamps was the lack of mosquitoes. They would've eaten them alive had it been warmer. The down side to this frigid water was the fact that he didn't know if his balls would ever thaw out. He found some humor in an impossible mathematical equation: how to get two very cold inches of penis through three inches of clothing when he had to pee.

The week passed quickly and without any formal ceremonies they returned to Camp McCall on their last day. They packed and returned to Fort Bragg. They loaded into the cattle cars—troop vehicles if you will. He caught a glimpse of the small TAC sergeant standing by the flagpole chewing his wad of tobacco. He waved as they left.

The conversation on the ride to Fort Bragg was light and good-humored. Everyone talked about a long hot shower, real food, beer, steak, getting laid, pizza, beer, getting laid, cornflakes and fried eggs, beer, getting laid, a real bed to sleep in, getting laid, a hot room with flushing toilets, and, of course most importantly, getting laid.

When they arrived at Fort Bragg he went to his newly assigned room. He quickly undressed and headed straight for the shower. After a month of cold showers and frigid swamp water, all he could think about was running the hot water over his body. Never had anything felt so good to him. After thirty minutes he felt almost clean but couldn't bring himself to leave the warm shower. The scabs on his back washed away. His open wounds started to bleed again, but it felt good! Finally he mustered up the strength to leave. He went back to his room and made his bed. He lay down on his belly and instantly fell asleep. The good food, the wine and women would have to wait for another day.

He had the weekend off. On Monday he would move from the old wooden billets to the new brick billets where he would stay for his phase two training. But for now he was off, and he wanted to get far away from the Army. He drove to the first decent motel he could find with cable TV. He went to his room and called her. She answered on the first ring.

"Hello?"

"Hi. Would you care to spend a little time with a guy who just wants to look at you and eat several steaks, a couple of big Macs, and a large chocolate shake?"

"Sounds good to me!" she said.

"Pick you up in thirty minutes?"

"Ok!" He hung up the phone with a smile, the first relaxed smile he had in a long time. It didn't seem natural on his face. He should have asked her if she had any corn flakes. His stomach growled its displeasure at missing breakfast. He had no intention of eating in the mess hall until he was forced to. She met him at the door with a big smile and a kiss. She pulled him inside, away from the cold wind. He said hello to her mom and dad. The two of them ran out the door as soon as the necessary pleasantries were completed. She placed her arm around his back and saw the pain flash across his face. She removed her arm and placed it through his. She wanted to do something to ease his pain but knew he would feel uncomfortable if she tried.

They spent the day together, laughing and carefree. They were in love. Eating was the serious part of his day, and watching him eat was the humorous part for her. It amazed her how much food he packed away. He ordered a twenty-ounce steak with fries, drank six cups of coffee, had a slice of German chocolate cake, a blackberry cobbler pie with ice cream, then ordered a hamburger to go with the works! They took in a movie. He ate two bags of popcorn and downed a large soda. Then he fell into a post-Thanksgiving slumber. She had to wake him up several times because he was snoring. After the movie, they stopped at another restaurant. He ate again. She stared at him. Where was he putting all that food?

The day ended abruptly. He drove her home. He wished that he could take her to his motel room instead. She wanted to stay with him, but neither of them had the courage to say how they were really feeling. He kissed her goodnight. He drove to a fast food restaurant. He ordered a large hamburger, fries, a chocolate shake, and a cherry pie. He drank several more cups of coffee before turning in. That night his mother came to him in his dreams. She was smiling and saying something he could not understand. He asked her to show him what it was that made her so happy. She laughed. It was the first time since he was a child that he could hear it! It made him swell with happiness. She beckoned, and there beside her stood his father!

Phase two began with eight hours of classes and four hours of homework. Most of the engineer classes were on construction—how to build roads, airfields, buildings, and concrete cement mixing. All of this was just a review for him. He was already trained as a combat engineer. The formulas for explosives were easy to grasp and so was the analytical weight classification of bridges. There were several field exercises that separated them for a week at a time. His back had recovered but left several scars to remind him of the rucksack runs. He was up to seven miles a day on his morning runs.

Before he was ready, phase two was completed, and he was on his way back to Camp McCall for his last four weeks of training.

Phase three consisted of some classified classes followed by two weeks in the woods putting it all together. They worked with civilians and soldiers from other units, quickly forming an effective guerilla fighting force. They had saved the easiest training for last. His four weeks passed so smoothly he almost had regrets of leaving.

Graduation day! They were back from Camp McCall and all dressed in their khaki uniforms. He felt an immense pride as he walked across the stage to receive his diploma. He looked for her in the crowd of happy faces. He scanned the audience until he found her. She was sitting with her parents, beaming with pride. He felt so proud at this time to be an American. His only regret was that his father and mother were not there to share this with him.

He was assigned to Seventh Special Forces Group. He walked into the orderly room of the old-style wooden barracks. He was introduced to his company sergeant major who in turn introduced him to his company commander. He was mildly surprised when they asked him what team he would like to be placed on. They gave him the option of mountain, halo, or scuba. He chose the mountain team. The idea of falling thirty thousand feet from an aircraft or swimming for miles under water did not appeal to him. It sent butterflies through his stomach just thinking about it. No, he would keep his feet on nice solid ground if that were possible.

The company sergeant major drove him over to the team house to meet everyone. As he entered the two-story wooden billet, the team's senior medic yelled, "Hey Top! Would you suck a man's dick for a million dollars?"

"Hell no," said his new team sergeant without hesitation. "I wouldn't do it for two million!"

"How can you be so sure?" asked the medic.

"Cause I might like it," his team sergeant replied. "And I don't want to go around kicking myself in the ass for not doing it before now." The sergeant major made the introductions and wished him good luck. He shook his hand and left. He was shown a wooden locker marked "senior engineer" before the team sergeant briefed him on the team's mission. As the briefing came to a close, the remainder of the team came in. More introductions followed. They all welcomed him with eyes that told him he would have to prove himself before he would be accepted as a member of this team. Little did he know at the time that he would spend the next eight years of his life with these men.

They were short a medic and a communications man. He was number ten of a twelve-man team. Of all the team members, he turned out to be the second shortest in stature. The senior communications man was about two inches shorter. Everyone else, he noted, was between five-foot-eight and five-foot-ten with the exception of the light weapons man. He was six-foot-five in stocking feet and tipped the scales at 250 pounds. He was a big black man with a twisted sense of humor. They would become good friends. The weeks passed quickly, and with the cold weather approaching their physical training increased. They ran five miles every morning, followed by hand-to-hand combat or an upper or lower body burn out. The rest of the day was spent in a classroom environment, giving classes to each other on their special skills. He set up demolition training, and they spent a week on the demolition range blowing up old pickup trucks and steel I-beams from old bridges.

They flew to Colorado where he had his first rough terrain jump. He wore a suit that resembled a mechanic's coveralls with padding in the knees and elbows. It had a special foam strap that covered the most important area—between his legs. He also wore a leather helmet with a wire mesh face shield in front. The flight called for them to rig in flight and conduct a night jump into the mountains. There would be no flat piece of sandy ground for a drop zone this time. It was dark by the time they started to put on their parachutes and attach their rucksacks to the harness just below the reserve. The glow of the interior lights cast a greenish haze through the aircraft. It gave him a sense of traveling in a spaceship. The dim figures of his teammates shifted and moved back and forth with the plane's movements.

They pushed a bundle containing their extra rations and batteries. The bundle was highly important since they would be in the mountains for a month. The bundle would go out first, and the team's executive officer would jump next, following the bundle to the ground. Then the team would link up with him.

He could feel the knots jumble in his stomach. The jump commands came at a rapid pace. First the bundle and then the XO left the aircraft. He shuffled forward as each man disappeared from the plane. His movements were somewhat restricted by the 150 pounds of extra weight. His rucksack was packed full of ropes and carabiners, extra clothing, a sleeping bag, food to last two weeks, and extra radio batteries. It rested on top of his jungle boots and made it impossible for him to jump. All he could do was shuffle slowly towards the door of the aircraft and fall forward.

His first jump with the team would become the standard for all future exits from the aircraft. He could not jump up and out as he had been trained to do with all the weight he was carrying. He took the door position and leaned forward, falling face first at attention. He tumbled into the frigid night air. The wire mesh face cover didn't permit him to see the ground or the other jumpers. He lifted the wire mesh with one hand. Unveiled to him was a world for which he had been longing. The clear Colorado sky was strewn with millions of stars. They appeared so close that he could almost touch them. The sharp, high peaks of the snow-covered mountains and white clouds above surrounded him. His awe of Mother Nature ended abruptly when he realized that he was falling entirely too fast. The high altitude and cold night temperature made the most bone-jarring landing he had experienced to date.

He had been lucky and found a small patch of clearing into which he managed to steer his chute. And he just missed several large trees. He came in running with the wind and, upon impact with the ground, had the air knocked out of him. He lay still for a few seconds, afraid to move lest he discover a broken leg or back. He wiggled his toes and methodically moved each part of his body until he was reassured that nothing serious was broken. Other than a few bruises, he was fine. As the air returned to his reluctant lungs, he stood slowly. He breathed more deeply, relieving his starved lungs with air. He rolled his parachute and placed it into the kit bag. Thirty minutes later, all team members were assembled in the same clearing, and they moved out into the frosty night.

They spent a month in the mountains. His team taught him climbing techniques and their standard operating procedures for each man as well as their responsibilities while moving through the woods. They also demonstrated the various ambushes they might encounter and how to deal with each one. They drilled tirelessly until each man knew precisely what to do in any given situation. To his surprise, he realized he had a great deal of knowledge to share with his team. The other men knew the basics of survival when it came to building traps and snares, but he heightened their level of expertise by sharing the ways of his mother's people.

By the time they departed Colorado, he had become a lead climber on the team. He had tremendous upper body strength and a light body weight which enabled him to negotiate with ease on overhangs and cliffs. He was scared several times when he fell, but the weapon's man stopped his fall each time. The big guy threatened to "whoop" his ass if he did it again.

His team had started to accept him as a member of their tight-knit group. And just as important, he was starting to accept them. There were no remarks about his heritage, just good humor about his ability or lack of it. They were good soldiers who gave each other a hard time to lighten the mood.

They jumped into Fort Bragg in the late afternoon. Trucks were waiting to take them back to the team house. They unloaded all the equipment, cleaned their rifles, and got an accountability on all their equipment before they were released for a four-day pass. He took another long, hot shower. He scrubbed himself red with a brush until he thought the skin would come off. Both of his shoulders were black and blue from his rucksack. He was thankful that he did not have any sores on his back this time. He went to his room and put on his favorite pair of blue jeans and a short-sleeve shirt. The softness of civilian clothes was an almost forgotten memory. The tennis shoes on his feet felt light and comfortable like they did when he was a little boy.

She answered on the second ring. "What took you so long to answer?" She laughed with that magical laugh he had longed to hear for the past thirty days. Yes, she would love to have dinner. Yes, he could pick her up now! Yes, she still loved him! He could not get enough of her kisses. He said kissing her was like trying to eat just one potato chip. You can't stop with just one. She told him she had taken off for the weekend anticipating his return.

They drove to Myrtle Beach and spent the weekend together. They were alone for the first time since they had started dating. They made love to each other over and over again. A mixture of pure lust and love flooded their senses. His need for food was the only thing that forced them apart, and then only for the time it took to eat. Then it was back to the motel for more love-making.

The TV never came on; the phone did not ring. It was the best weekend of his life. For the first time he was happy. He honestly felt he had met the woman with whom he would spend the rest of his life. She lay sleeping in his arms. Her soft breathing moved his chest hairs in a gentle rhythm. He pulled her hair back gently to get a better look at her face. He tried to visualize her in her seventies and eighties and could not see anything but the young delightful face before him. He knew no matter how old she became, she would always look like she did at this moment to him. Yes, he thought, she is the one.

CHAPTER 9

1971

After thirty days in the mountains he was in good shape but not as good as he needed to be for the next phase of their work. He spent weeks getting in shape only to go to the woods for months at a time with no running involved. Then he had to return to Fort Bragg and be expected to complete the five-mile run through the North Carolina sand. Falling in and out of tip-top shape became his normal pattern. He had completed his first year on the A-team and had finally been accepted as a bonafide team member. They had traveled to Colorado, California, Hawaii, and Australia.

That year he was selected by the Department of the Army for promotion to sergeant first class. He was happy to see that he was number seven on a list of eight hundred promotions. He wondered who the six ahead of him were. In a short seven years he had become a Vietnam veteran, an instructor, a drill sergeant, and a Green Beret. He was twenty-six years old, and he knew in the past year he had changed. He knew in his heart he had changed for the better because of her and his team. He now had a place in the world. He had something he sought for his entire life: a place to belong, a place where he was welcomed and needed. He felt something he had not experienced until now. He felt like a man.

He was there the day she graduated from nursing school, when she walked up to receive her diploma. After a celebratory dinner with her family and a few close friends, they drove to Myrtle Beach. They booked a room in a hotel on the coast. The next three days were filled with swimming, deep conversations, and love-making until they fell asleep. They awoke just as the sun was blinking its goodbyes on their last day. After sharing a pizza, they walked along the boardwalk holding hands. They watched the angry ocean sending one white cap wave after another along the beach. A cool breeze kicked up, and she nestled herself closer to him. Her arms entwined around his as they walked slowly to the end of the boardwalk. They had the boardwalk to themselves, and the two of them stood leaning over the rail tasting the salty air on their lips. After several minutes of listening to the sea rolling in she asked him, "What are you thinking about?"

"Well I'm thinking about finding a good woman, getting married, and raising a family. Did you have any girlfriends that might be interested?" He received a poke on the arm.

He pulled out the set of rings for which he had been saving money during the past year. He placed it on her finger with the words, "I have never known anyone who could make me feel so complete and whole as I do when I'm with you, and I want to spend the rest of my life with you." She cried. They hugged and kissed and cried together. Time itself slipped away. Neither of them wanted to break the spell that encircled them. They stood holding each other until the early rays of morning beckoned. She caught a strange look on his face as though listening and looking far away. He couldn't explain it to her. He was unable to express how happy the spirits were for them. He couldn't see them, but he knew they were dancing.

CHAPTER 10

Big mistake, he kept saying over and over again under his breath. What had ever possessed him to agree to his teammates throwing a bachelor party in his honor? Now he found himself in his current and rather embarrassing predicament. He awoke from a deep sleep to find he was sitting on a park bench beside the bus station. He assumed it was Fayetteville, North Carolina. No, he started to pray it was Fayetteville, North Carolina. Knowing his team, it was quite possible that he was in another state or for that matter another country. Both of his legs were in a cast from the ankle to his thighs. He was wearing a military raincoat with his hands placed through the pocket slits and handcuffed together in front of him. On his feet was a pair of shower shoes. But other than that, he was completely naked. He moved his hands slightly against his belly and discovered he had been shaved from his chest down. After slowly moving his hands downward he found his fears were well-founded. They had shaved the pubic hairs completely around his balls and his ass. He found a quarter taped to his right hand. But in order to use it he would have to raise both hands. In doing so he would lift the raincoat and thereby expose him and his bald buddy to the world.

As his luck would have it, his small world was becoming more populated by the minute. A greyhound bus from Charleston had just pulled into the parking lot beside him. What had the medic slipped into his drink? The fog was now rapidly leaving his brain. He remembered being at his team sergeant's house. Everyone was having a good time. Each team member took turns toasting him and his future bride. There was the expected team banter. The guys drew numbers to see which one was going to be the first to sleep with his wife for him on his wedding night. He remembered a porno flick and the heavy weapons man giving him a class on how to eat pussy like a black man.

The communications sergeant disagreed with everything the big guy was telling him.

"No! No! Man, listen to me. You want to knock on it just one time you understand? Sure you can do it five or six times in one night for a night or two. What you gonna do when she gets used to it, and you can't hang? 'Course I can because it's in my blood, man. But you being white or whatever, hell, there's no way you can stand on it every night like I do."

"She will get used to it and expect that every night, and you gotta know from past experience that you just can't hang, man. It just ain't in your genes." Then nothing. Whatever was in his drink had laid him out cold. He shuddered, thinking about a drunken medic shaving around his balls with a razor. The rest of the team must have put the casting material on his legs. Good job, he thought, but a lot thicker than any cast should be.

People were unloading off the bus and throwing glances his way. What to do, what to do. Some of the more unsavory characters were checking him out for the possibility of a permanent loan. He could tell by their huddle and indirect glances his way they were thinking of his wallet. Well, I suppose that's the good news. Don't have it with me. Then frowning, he wondered where it was along with the rest of his clothing. He was thinking about trying to stand up, but knew if he fell, he could not regain his feet. The visual image of falling and exposing himself to the now more frequent looks did not appeal to him. The leg casts were a good two inches thick and completely dry. There was no way he would be able to bend his knees or keep his balance. He had to pee. The urgency so strong it made his teeth hurt.

A Fayetteville patrol car came cruising slowly through the bus parking lot. The police officer glanced over at him with a somewhat stern look on his face. Well here goes something. He yelled at the top of his voice, "Help! Police! I'm in distress!" He caught the eye of the police officer and yelled even louder. "Help! I'm a soldier in distress!" The patrol car pulled over several feet away from him, and the officer cautiously got out of his car. He proceeded to walk towards him. Several of the spectators that had been sizing him up for a loan walked away swiftly in the other direction. The officer, a somewhat pudgy individual, came up and stood in front of him. He looked like he'd been on the force long enough to have a sense of humor. Well, time to find out. "Hello, officer! I trust you are having a pleasant evening. I must apologize for the inconvenience, but I was wondering if you might assist me to the bathroom and then perhaps make a phone call for me?"

"What's your problem?" the officer demanded in a very authoritarian voice. He maintained a distance of five feet from him.

"Well, sir! I have to pee so bad my teeth are floating. My legs are in full-length casts that I, as far as I know, do not need. My hands are cuffed inside this raincoat, but if I raise them to show you I will expose a freshly shaved body that, from my calculations, goes from my neck to well past, but includes my buddy and his two sidekicks. I trust you will believe me when I say I did not have any say in this matter. And, no, sir! I am not drunk, nor am I hallucinating. I do pray however that this is all a very bad dream." The patrolman's face, cautious and alert up to this point, slowly turned to one of amusement. He cracked out in a laugh, softly at first. But as he stood there looking at the man in a raincoat with both legs in a full cast sitting on a bench beside the bus station at two o'clock in the morning, his small laugh gradually gained tempo until it was an outright belly roar. The poor cop laughed so hard he had to place both hands on his knees to support himself. Then, after several moments, he regained his composure and pulled out his flashlight. Slowly, he eased himself down to one knee and lifted the corner of the raincoat with his nightstick. More fitful laughter filled the night air as the policeman used his flashlight beam to confirm the story he had just heard.

As he wiped his eyes with the back of each hand, the patrolman said in between his hysterical laughter, "I will be right back." He headed to his patrol car. Then over his shoulder he yelled, "Don't go anywhere!" Another fit of uncontrollable laughter bent him over at the waist.

"Damn it!" He said to himself. He overheard the patrolman on the radio telling the dispatcher in between fits of laughter to send all available patrol cars to the bus station. He knew that the one thing that would get cops to a scene as fast as "officer down" would be something this outrageously funny.

"Didn't take five minutes," he mumbled in a demoralized tone. The parking lot must have every cop and state highway patrol car within a fifty-mile radius sitting in it. All of them were standing around him in a circle asking question after question, howling at his direct and matter-of-fact answers.

"When are you getting married?" He was asked for the umpteenth time.

"Tomorrow morning, sir!" More belly laughs. Flashlights were gleaming up the front of his raincoat. Each officer in line took his turn to glance under his raincoat. Each officer went into a fit of hysteria.

"What's she gonna think when she sees that?" asked one young rookie cop before lifting the raincoat for another look.

"Probably have me move back into the barracks until the hair grows out," he replied in a sad, defeated voice. Cameras were being brought out of the patrol cars in rapid succession. Not exactly what he wanted to see. After several officers helped him to his feet, they took turns getting their picture taken with him. Finally, on his threat to piss there on the pavement, they walked him toward the bus station. A mixture of more howls followed him as he was led away on legs that were spread out at exaggerated angles. What now? A gentle breeze drifted across his backside. The bastards had cut a circle from the back of the raincoat which now exposed his buttocks. Some of the cops had fallen down with uncontrollable laughter. Had there been an emergency at that moment, there was no way they could have responded. About fifty people from the bus station were howling in unison with the cops.

"Glad I can bring so much joy into so many dull lives," he whispered under his breath. He came out of the bathroom, and one of the officers removed his handcuffs. The patrol cars were in the process of leaving. They waved with one hand and continued to wipe tears out of their eyes with the other. He was left standing with the first officer on the scene.

"Would you like a lift?" the officer asked.

"To the emergency room in the hospital at Fort Bragg," he replied in a grateful voice. The officer helped him lie down in the back seat, lifting his legs so they rested against the door window. All he could see was flashing red lights on his way to the hospital. The officer looked over his shoulder from time to time which brought on another continuous stream of laughter. The hospital staff went through the same unhinged amusement and questioning. After everyone in the hospital had come down to the emergency room to get an eyeful, he was finally led into a small room where the leg casts were removed. Coming out of the room, he was mildly surprised to see the police officer still there. He was offered a lift home, which he gratefully accepted. The officer dropped him off at his barracks and shook his hand. He told him he wished him the best of luck with a sincere, straight face. He cracked up one last time before he hurriedly drove away.

He tiptoed into the barracks past a sergeant doing the charge of quarters duty. He tried to casually stroll by as though he was not in a raincoat with his ass sticking out. He heard a chuckle behind him, and someone began whistling the Navy tune, "*Anchors Away.*" His last thoughts before going to sleep were deep in the planning stages of how he would get even with his team members. It would take him a long time, and it would require a lot of thought. He would spend hours in preparation, but if it was the last thing he did on this earth, he would get even.

1972 His son was born. He had come home from a short training mission to find her gone. It was three o'clock in the morning, and a note was on the door. "Everything is ok. Just having your baby! See you when you get here."

He forced himself to stay within the posted speed limits on his way to the hospital. Was she alright? What would he ever do without her? Would the baby be normal? The thoughts running through his mind were those all expectant fathers asked. He raced up to the maternity ward.

The nurse smiled as he came through the door. She told him what he wanted to hear on their way to his wife's room.

"You have a beautiful, chubby boy!" He was shown to her room.

"Hi. I'm all right. And our son is all right . . . in fact he is perfect, perfect down to his toes. I'm exhausted, but other than that the birth went smoothly." He stayed with her, holding her hand and whispering, "I love you. I love you. I love. . . ." He kept saying it as she drifted off to sleep. When they brought his son in for his feeding, he took the small, gurgling baby from the nurse and held him. He was so afraid the boy would break. He was still red, and his crying made his little face even redder.

He had taken his son outside on his first night home and held him up to the sky, offering thanks to the Creator as his father had done with him under his mother's guidance. For a short period of time as he stood there with his son held above his head, he felt at one with the universe. At the same time he felt small and insignificant in the vastness of time and space. But above all, he was extremely happy, even though for the first time in his life he feared his own mortality.

"You waste more diapers!" His wife complained. Each time one of his teammates stopped by, he had to remove the diaper to show off his sons huge balls.

"Just look at those, would you," he bragged. "They are almost as big as his old man's." Of course there were several comments on his son's penis size being slightly larger as well. He passed out cigars as only a proud father can do. He insisted on the two o'clock feedings. This was his time to spend with just the boy, as he had started calling him instead of his name.

His wife was all too happy to give him the early morning feeding. His son had been born at the perfect time. There were no missions scheduled, and they were in training. He attended NBC school—nuclear, biological, and chemical school. Mostly classroom instruction, it left his evenings free to be with his family. They had moved into government quarters on post so he had a ten-minute ride to work. She stayed home for the first six weeks after her delivery. On the morning she was supposed to go back to work at the hospital, he found her sitting at the kitchen table crying. His concern diminished into relief as she explained between sobs that she could not leave their son at the daycare. She was sorry, but would he mind if she stayed home for a little longer? He kissed away her tears and told her how happy it actually made him. He had been worried for days about the boy being in a strange place.

Life had never been so wonderful! He went to work and came home every night, just like a civilian. The two of them were wrapped in a world of their own. They were fascinated by how fast their son was growing. Her parents could not stay away. They stopped by every day, bringing gifts and checking to see what new thing the boy was doing.

There were no missions for three blessed months. He watched his son grow by leaps and bounds. He could not hold him or play with him enough. The day he was born he had gone to see the supply sergeant and told him he wanted a Green Beret for his son.

"What size?" asked the supply sergeant. Thinking on his toes he responded, "The smallest one available." The sergeant handed him a size six and a half. When he made the trip to the hospital that afternoon, he placed the beret in his son's crib. To his dismay he realized that the beret was almost half as big as the boy was.

"No problem, boy," he said. "You will just have to grow a little." As he was leaving the hospital, he saw another new dad rush in with a brand new tricycle. Some guys are idiots. His son's Green Beret now hung above the crib. Three happy months. Then, all too soon it came to an end. A phone call came at 0300 hours. The code word told him this was a live mission.

He kissed his wife deeply, and he kissed his son. He breathed in the baby smell to keep him in his thoughts. His heart broke as he left the two of them standing in the door. The boy was asleep in his wife's arms.

"Two months of bull shit," he said to himself. They had deployed in a small African country to a branch of the African army that could not read or write. His mission was to teach them advanced demolitions. It was something he wasn't even permitted to teach American soldiers, but his country could send him halfway around the world to teach demolitions to other soldiers. Hope they don't blow me up with them!

Still there had to be a reason. His government wouldn't send him halfway around the world without a good reason. There were no toilet facilities or adequate water for drinking. The medic kept busy with dysentery and other strange illnesses that each team member developed.

Several years earlier, Special Forces soldiers had trained the man who now held power as president of this country. Now they were back to train a new generation of soldiers for the newly-elected president at his request. The Army deemed this an important mission because there were now no soldiers in the country who had received training from the United States Special Forces. And that was primarily because the newly-elected president had executed everyone else who had undergone training by Special Forces when he overthrew the previous regime.

Late at night there was machine gun fire along the perimeter. They thought they were under attack. The team prepared to deploy into the area. Later they learned that the men on guard duty were merely scared and had fired their guns to chase away evil spirits.

One African soldier had broken his femur bone the day after they had arrived. The medic had done an excellent job of setting it and transporting him to his village about ten miles away. Through the interpreter, the medic explained to the family that the cast had to stay on for at least six weeks. Thirty days later the soldier came walking into camp! When the medic asked him what had happened to his cast, the soldier explained that the village witch doctor had come in right after his departure and removed it. The witch doctor took a live chicken and broke one of its legs. The soldier had been informed by the witch doctor, "When chicken walk, you walk." The man had walked the ten miles to the base camp to get paid. His leg was bowed and shorter than the other one. Now he walked with a lopsided gate, but he was walking.

He had to be inventive when training the African soldiers. He also had to watch them extremely closely. Sometimes they would do something, thinking they were helping him out when they were really making things much worse. One time they threw his blasting caps on top of a couple of boxes of explosives. Or they did things like seeing who could be first to light their fuses even though they were still holding blocks of TNT in their hands. Somehow he managed to train them without any casualties or getting himself killed.

His wife greeted him at the door. She held his son in one arm as she reached out to hold him with the other. She gave him a much-needed and long-awaited kiss. His son looked at him for a split second then virtually leaped from his mother's arm towards him. This became the normal lifestyle for his family: long trips in other countries doing whatever was asked of him, then returning home to a quiet life. Quiet until the next mission took him away.

He saw death in various stages on many of these extended trips. He saw miles of grain rotting on the docks, rats by the thousands eating food sent to help the starving masses, governments refusing to give food to their own people in fear of it making the people strong enough to overthrow their political regime. He saw kids of all ages dying from disease and famine. He saw a young mother carrying a dead child about the same age as his son. It devastated him. It made him crazy to see people starve while a select few drove in limousines and ate exotic meals and gave parties that could have fed half the country they controlled. He found it difficult to eat with so much misery around him. He sought out a place to hide from starving eyes whenever he ate. Each bite of food he ingested in these African countries tugged at his conscience. It filled him with more fuel to return home; at the same time it made him feel sick. His team members fared no better. They couldn't comprehend the amount of evil or greed that lead to so much suffering.

Each time he returned home to his family, it took several days for him to adjust, to return to his old self and carry on a sense of normality with his wife and son. It became a ritual.

There were several years when he was away for more than ten months out of the year. Most of his missions kept him away for at least six months. Each time, on his return home he was shocked by the growth spurts his son had gone through while he was away.

He felt guilty about the time he spent away from his family. He knew he could never make up every Christmas, birthday, or soccer game. He thought on several occasions of leaving the Army, of becoming a civilian and getting a job where he could be with them every night. But he was afraid. The Army had accepted his Indian heritage without question. The Army had been his salvation and given him opportunities to succeed. He couldn't imagine subjecting his family to the life he once led. As a soldier he was treated as an equal. Out there in the civilian world it might be much different. He knew he would harm anyone that would insult his family. He knew in his heart that the Army had become his protector.

In order for him to be treated with respect he would have to be in the Army—until the day came when there was no more hate and evil. That would be a long time. His travels around the world confirmed this. There was more than enough hate and greed to last.

1977

His team sergeant broke the news to them. Special Forces would soon be a memory. The president of the United States no longer saw the need for them.

"The president believes we are a thing of the past and in order to save money, he has cut our budget. He thinks that satellites in the sky can do the same job of surveillance. There is no longer a need for unconventional warfare experts to train on today's modern battlefield. Don't give up hope though," said the team sergeant. "We have some pretty powerful friends in Congress who are trying to talk some sense into that man."

After months of uncertainty, it finally became official. One A-team per company was to be disbanded. The men sat in stony silence and disbelief. How did the president reach such a disastrous conclusion?

The next two years were the worst years in his military career. There were few real missions. There was no ammunition to practice their patrol techniques. The men were reduced to play soldiers as they pointed empty rifles and yelled, "Bang, bang!" There was no money to replace equipment or buy explosives to train. He was reduced to giving demolition classes using blocks of clay representing blocks of explosives, with string for the time fuse. Perhaps the worst thing that happened for his team was their primary surveillance.

"If I had wanted to be a damn recon idiot, I would have joined the Marines," he heard his weapon's man say one day after watching a toad move across a secluded highway. Hidden in a spot that gave them just enough room to lie down, they were counting vehicles.

Throughout the company more and more financial restrictions were placed on them. A lot of them felt that if this guy got re-elected, they would get out of the Army. He never said it himself, but he wouldn't reenlist.

The Iran rescue mission had the worst effect on morale for all of them. What was that idiot thinking? Instead of allowing Delta Force to do their jobs, he had maintained a micro-management chokehold on the mission. The president had insisted that all branches of the service participate in the hostage rescue attempt. Men who had never served together or trained together were thrown into a mission that had almost no chance of success. He believed the president designed the hostage rescue attempt for political purposes. He wanted to give credit to all the branches. Too bad his brilliant mind could not foresee the aftermath of his blunder. Some very good and brave men were dead, and for what reason? And the hostages were still hostages. Hell, any two A-teams could have completed the job, or even the Rangers, or Marine recon.

He just hoped to God this fiasco would't take any of their lives.

How many days had it been since he had slept? The thought came from somewhere in the far recess of his mind. He willed one foot in front of the other as he tried to calculate the days without food or rest. The small animal trail they had been on since daybreak was leading them in the general direction of the pick-up point. The junior medic stumbled in front of him, weaving at times like a drunken sailor. They had at least eight more kilometers to go.

Each man knew if the chopper did not meet them this time, they would all die. Or worse, be taken prisoner. He had never pushed his body or mind to these limits before. Three days—was that how long he had been walking?

The Iranian guards had been captured without a single bullet being fired. The secret communications and satellite dishes had been dismantled. They had moved to their pick-up point without incident. They had made communications with their support elements for evacuation. The mission had been a success. They were waiting for the arrival of the C-130 to retrieve them and their equipment. The Iranian guards that sat bound and gagged would be released as soon as they boarded the aircraft.

The mission was almost over when everything turned to shit. The Russian helicopter coming in their direction contained a relief force of Iranians. From their concealed position, they observed the military force unload and start searching for their location.

Somehow they had been compromised. Had the Russians told the Iranians they where there?

The mission had been simple enough. They had flown within twenty miles of the site. The C-130 landed on a dirt road just long enough for the aircraft to stop. Minutes after touchdown the aircraft had been airborne again and had flown out of sight. It had been almost dark as the aircraft made its departure. It had flown low to avoid Iranian radar. He had dreaded to see the plane bank and disappear behind a mountain peak.

They had moved out in single file, the team traveling at a snail's pace up the steep mountain. Their destination was a small listening station along the Iranian-Soviet border. The new regime in Iran had made this trip necessary. The sensitive listening devices were state of the art. The United States did not want these spy tools falling into enemy hands. There was a lot of concern that the Russians may have already got their hands on them. Each man on the team breathed a sigh of relief when they saw the station. In the soft twilight they could confirm that it was still operational. A lone Iranian soldier stepped outside of the small building and urinated. As soon as he walked back inside, they moved out swiftly and silently. The team surrounded the building. The team sergeant and the weapons man entered the door. The three men inside were taken completely by surprise and gave up without a fight.

He set demolition charges on the equipment too big for them to carry. They took the bound Iranian soldiers and made a quick departure out of the area. The force of the explosion passed them and echoed loudly through the mountains. A look through his star-light scope confirmed that the building was completely destroyed. The mission had gone like clockwork until the chopper showed up just minutes ahead of the C-130. Another chopper could be heard in the far distance.

"Let's kill these guys and get the hell out of here, Top," said the weapon's man. He glanced over at the two captured prisoners they still had with them. The team sergeant smiled and informed everyone that he would never be brought up on war crimes. They would secure the two prisoners and leave them. If they worked at it, they would eventually get loose. They left them gagged and bound to an old tree off the trail far enough so that they could not be seen. The hills were now infested with Iranians searching for them.

The political overthrow of the Shah of Iran had caught everyone off guard. The Iranians had captured the telecommunication site and ordered the United States Air Force personnel to leave. Some of the Iranian soldiers had worked with the Air Force on this site for years and had made friends with them. The soldiers they had captured at the site were new replacements. The old guards had been ordered back to their units for a loyalty evaluation to the new regime.

Their mission had been simple and direct: Go into Iran, retrieve what equipment they could, and destroy the rest before Russia could send their troops in and confiscate it.

Now the medic veered off the trail and fell to his knees in front of him. As he passed the medic he whispered, "It's easy to stay awake. All you need is a stick of gum." The medic looked at him confused. His mouth was wide open in a silent scream, and there was no sense of recognition in his eyes. He stumbled past the medic, not capable of thinking to help him up or offer him a stick of gum. His mind was beyond the threshold of thinking rationally. He managed to drag his feet for another hundred yards before he fell asleep walking. He tumbled to the ground. His senses returned to him. A loud buzzing noise was coming from somewhere.

He was on his knees. He saw the medic move past him. He was confused. The gum had been his secret weapon against falling asleep, and now it had failed him? He stayed on his knees trying to rationalize this bit of information. He could see his team members going up a small incline. Saw them as they stumbled and fell. He did not have the strength to move. He would just rest for a few more minutes. His ears filled with a high screeching noise. One pick-up point after another had been canceled. They were deep in the mountains now. No possibility of a C-130 landing as originally planned.

The Iranians were still looking for them. Several times a chopper had been en route to retrieve them. A dust storm canceled the first, and enemy activity within a hundred meters of them had cancelled the second. Each time they were forced to move deeper into the mountains to avoid the enemy. A nagging fear came over him. He had to get up and move. His team was now several hundred yards in front of him, and he might not be able to catch up with them. He forced his exhausted limbs to move. He struggled to his feet. Getting mad at himself for his weakness, he began a slow shuffle and made his last-ditch effort to catch up with his team. The top of a small knoll was their final destination. A chopper was supposed to pick them up. They were less than 300 yards from the hilltop. The medic fell again in front of him. This time he stopped and helped him up. They walked side by side the rest of the way. They drew strength from each other to reach the rest of their team.

Some of the men were about halfway to the top. The hill wasn't all that steep, but no one had any reserve strength left. Each man began to crawl on their hands and knees. He continued to walk and passed several who had started their slow, exhausted crawl. He fell again. This time he knew he could not stand. A sense of helplessness almost overwhelmed him. He barely had the will to crawl. The top of the hill was just a short distance from him, yet the amount of energy needed to reach the top made him feel small and insignificant.

He passed the team sergeant and heard him crying in deep-rooted frustration. Only then did he realize he was sobbing like a baby. There were no tears. His body had no moisture to give. Complete and total hopelessness enveloped his being. A 300-meter hill had transformed into an insurmountable obstacle. Every man wondered if they could make it. No one was capable of helping anybody else. They would be left behind if the rescue chopper didn't see them. They would be captured and put on public display by an angry mob of Iranians, then perhaps shot.

He would never be taken prisoner. He would rather die than undergo the barbaric torture and humiliation those bastards dealt out. He wanted to see his wife and son again. He wondered what they were doing. What time was it there? He used the wonderful memories of them to occupy his tortured mind, to take his mind from doing what he knew was impossible, to keep moving. He stopped crawling. He lifted his head up to see how much further he had to go. His eyes stung. They went in and out of focus for a minute—about 100 meters. It hurt to blink. A thick crust of dried mucus made his lids feel heavy and sore.

Others were now passing him. He began to crawl with thoughts of his son. He wanted to see him one more time. Please, God, give me the strength. A convulsion came over him. His arms collapsed. He could go no further. He dozed. The images of the kids who used to torment him in school filtered through his mind. "Stupid Indian!" they laughed. They laughed because he couldn't move up a small hill.

He felt the sting of the paddle. The words of the principal as he told him he would never amount to anything, “Look at you! You're still poor! You can't even climb a little hill! Look at my son. See how fast he can run up that small distance? He's better than you could ever dream to be. He's better than your son! You stupid Indian! Low life! Lay there and die!” He screamed and jerked himself awake. He wouldn't fall asleep again. He forced his body up and began to inch on his belly. A few inches at a time. He picked out a spot in front of him and willed his body to get to it.

They had been going for more than three days without sleep or water. They had traveled over a hundred miles through enemy-infested hills and valleys. Now their salvation was this small hilltop. If they were not evacuated here, death or the enemy would find them.

“I'm on top!” Someone yelled down to them. The last bit of will power ignited, and he moved more rapidly. When he had reached the top of the hill, he crawled to his position. He, like the other men, got to their positions on instinct from their years of training. Somehow, they set up a 360-degree defensive perimeter. He looked around and didn't see a chopper. He looked up at the sky and prayed to the Creator to help them.

“Prove that principal wrong, God.” He passed out. Someone was shaking him. He tried to fight them off. Anger built up inside of him. He forced his eyes open and stared blankly at a pilot. A crewman was screaming at him. What was he saying? He couldn't hear. He wanted to tell the guy to shut those damn engines off so he could hear. Through red, gritty eyes he could see members of his team being carried to a helicopter. He felt hands loosening his shoulder straps and removing his rucksack. He was lifted to his feet and onto the shoulders of two men. They dragged him to the chopper. He was thrown inside next to his team leader. The rest of the men were already inside. They all sat staring blankly. He watched two pilots struggle with his rucksack. He wanted to laugh at the two men as they fumbled to pick it up. They strained to lift it and finally dragged it to the chopper.

His last conscious memory was seeing the small hill they had occupied covered by Iranians. Puffs of smoke shot from their gun barrels. They became smaller and smaller until they were tiny dots too far away. He remembered nothing about the flight. He had no memory of loading off the chopper or being ushered into a debriefing room. His only memory was a cup of coffee that somehow landed in his hand.

He slept soundly for twenty hours. When he finally woke up, he was sore and hungry. He was in a military bed with sheets and a pillow. How did he get here? He sat up. His muscles felt like they were held together with wire. His hands had been cleaned and bandaged as had his knees and ankles. A pair of hospital pants and a shirt were on a chair beside him. Every movement brought pain as he dressed. His feet were swollen, and the shower shoes he put on were a welcome relief.

He hobbled slowly from his room and saw a young sailor sitting at a small wooden desk near the end of the hallway. He was on board a ship.

"Hey! Welcome back!" The sailor said with a smile. "Most of your team is at the mess. There are two still in the sack. Man! You guys look like you've been put through the wringer!"

The young man gave him directions to the mess. He could only mumble a thank you as he departed for some chow. The sailor didn't realize how uncomfortable he had just made him feel. When a complete stranger tried to make him feel special, he felt uneasy about it. He had stopped feeling special when his mother died. The only people in his world who made him feel good about himself had been his team, his wife, and his son.

When he entered the mess hall, he saw his teammates sitting at a table. He nodded to them and proceeded to go through the chow line. A Navy cook stopped him and said, "Go have a seat with your friends, Sarge. I'll take your order from the table." He was grateful, yet embarrassed for the special attention—just like an officer in the British Army. He could sense the same thoughts from his team members as he took a seat.

"How's it going?" he whispered. He sipped a cup of precious coffee. By the time his food arrived, the two communication men that had been asleep came in bleary-eyed and confused.

He did a quick count and realized the team sergeant was missing.

"Where's Top?" he asked the senior medic.

"He's fine. I checked on him just a few minutes ago. He's getting his last bag of fluids. He wouldn't take an IV when we ran out of water. He ordered me to give it to you all and not to tell the team leader or he'd whip my ass." Relief washed over him. They all made it. His plate was piled high with food—way too much food—and he proceeded to eat all of it.

Two weeks later, he was home wrestling with the boy and listening to the news. The Iranian hostage crisis developed into a deeper mess of confusion for the American people. He sat enjoying the aroma and sounds emanating from the kitchen as his wife prepared dinner. His son sat on the couch beside him. The peaceful serenity of it all didn't seem real. He wondered about the Iranian guards they tied up and left. Had they managed to untie themselves, or did someone find them before they starved to death?

"Come and get it!" his wife hollered from the kitchen. She continued to scurry around in last-minute preparations. He got up from the couch. He tickled his son just to hear him laugh again. Then he swung him up on his bruised shoulders. He walked with heavy steps to the dining room.

1983

They had been stationed in Germany for the past year. The new assignment overseas meant a long overdue promotion. He was now a master sergeant in charge of an A-team. At times the responsibility seemed too overwhelming, but he had been trained by the best so his team was one of the best in the battalion.

The three of them settled in and enjoyed the neat, clean villages and small towns. The massive Bavarian mountains with snow-covered peaks seemed to beckon them. On weekends they would go hiking through the mountains, enjoying some of the most scenic country in the world. The casern where he was stationed had been built for the German SS soldiers in World War II. The air was full of history and mystique.

The post was set up in an ideal manner for Special Forces. Within minutes, they could climb some of the most difficult mountains. Some of the climbs would take the team an entire day to reach the top. Often they would camp overnight before heading down the next day. He enjoyed the evening talks around the campfire with his men.

The crisp night air was strewn with an uncountable number of stars. It gave him a feeling that all was as it should be. The view welcomed him the following morning. The sun brought into a view a number of endless sights. He would often sit on the edge of a cliff with his legs dangling over a shear drop of several thousand feet. He would be lost in meditation, recounting his blessings and feeling grateful to be alive, thanking the Great Spirit for his kindness bestowed upon him and his family.

During the winter months they went skiing on some of the best slopes in the world. His team had spent the past thirty days in the mountains. They were constantly testing new equipment the military needed in cold environments. The new equipment ranged from boots to sleeping bags and required testing in the worst possible conditions. The temperature would drop to sixty degrees below zero during the night. The new sleeping bags performed remarkably well given their light weight. Regardless, they were still cold. The chill seemed to set in their bones and remain there. Getting into their tents and zipping up the sleeping bag would bring just enough warmth to keep them alive.

He shared his tent with the team leader, a highly-motivated captain who was in top physical condition, but one who disliked cold weather. One night he was sound asleep and was awakened by a crushing force on top of him. His first thought had been an avalanche had trapped them. When the "avalanche" began to move he realized it was his team leader. "Sorry," said the team leader as he struggled to his feet. The guy was trying to stand up inside his sleeping bag. He hopped to the door of the tent. It became obvious to him moments later what he had in mind when he heard his team leader urinating. He was standing with his pecker hanging out of the door flaps peeing just outside the tent. They were testing an A-frame tent. One of the reasons they would give it a poor recommendation was because it was too high, and the silhouette would stand out bringing unwanted attention. The other reason was that it was cold! The height of the tent did not retain any body heat. There is nothing worse than being almost warm in a sleeping bag and having to listen to someone else pee. It's a mind thing, but when you hear someone else go in below zero weather, you have to go too.

He lay in his bag trying to go back to sleep, fighting the urge to pee. It was useless; there was no getting around it. He would have to get up and urinate. His bladder became fuller with each passing second. Not wanting to be a sissy like his team leader, he lay shivering in the sixty-below temperature. He thought for several minutes, I'm going to unzip this sleeping bag and jump out. I'm going to run outside and show this sorry excuse for a human how a real man can do this. He took a deep breath and unzipped his sleeping bag. He got his booties on, he was already starting to shiver. He jumped up and ran to the door.

"Oh, shit!" he said through clanking teeth. Even his eyeballs began to shake from the cold. The team leader had pissed on the zipper of the tent and it was now frozen solid! He stood there butt naked, trying to free the zipper. He knew he was in trouble. He went back to his bag and located his cigarette lighter in the dark. After several minutes he had the zipper free, and he could not wait any longer. He jumped outside of the tent peeing as he went. He stood in snow up to his knees. It seemed as though he wouldn't finish peeing before he froze to death. By the time he got back into his sleeping bag his teeth were chattering so fast he could barely talk. This did not prevent him from talking to his team leader who lay snoring softly in his bag. "Sssoorry mot-moth-motherfffffffffuuuuk!" He made a mental note to carry prophylactics with him in the future, which he did. He would pee in them and tie them in a knot. Then he'd place them gently under his team leader's head.

They would crawl out of their bags at 0200 hours in the morning to send a radio message, then remain standing during the coldest part of the night until they received a message from headquarters. By the time they crawled back into their sleeping bags, the stages of hypothermia were noticeable in all of them. He would lie shivering while eating a frozen candy bar to regain some inner body heat.

Each morning they would test the new stoves as they heated up the new generation of army rations. Then after packing everything into their rucksacks as fast as possible, they would spend the day traveling up and down the mountains. By mid-morning they were skiing in their underwear, sweat pouring off them in a cloud of steam. The view looked rather odd to him as he looked back to see his team behind him. The thin long johns were a lime-green color and gave them all the appearance of being Santa's little elves moving cheerfully through the snow.

He took his family skiing on weekends and by the end of the first season they were doing the black diamond slopes together. The winter passed all too quickly for him.

Spring found him in Greece, training the Greek army on advanced demolitions. He was upset with this type of an assignment. He didn't believe they should be teaching other soldiers their secrets on explosives, especially when they could turn around and use them in guerrilla warfare. He was never permitted to teach these secrets to American soldiers. Why then give something so dangerous to unstable third world countries? He did have to admit, the Greeks were really excellent soldiers.

The summer months passed with no missions to other parts of the world. His team spent their time brushing up on languages. His weekends were free. He took his family on long drives, exploring the surrounding countries of Austria, France, Belgium, Switzerland, and Italy. His life had never been more secure and happy. The boy grew like a weed and ate like a horse.

It started out as a routine training mission in Germany. The team was supposed to fly by chopper to the base of a mountain and spend the day climbing. But the helicopter crashed. They were about twenty feet from touching down when he had removed his seat belt. Seconds later the Huey started acting strange. A loud humming noise reverberated through his ears. He could see the pilot struggling with the controls. They were climbing higher, and the chopper was flying almost on its side, his side. They were gaining altitude. The trees were coming towards him. He was on the verge of jumping out when the pilot made a last ditch correction and swerved to miss the trees. The maneuver worked and saved the cab of the aircraft, but the tail section was torn off as were the main rotors. Everything began to move in slow motion. The chopper made its dying plunge toward the ground from eighty feet in the air, crashing nose first into a small opening in the forest. He was thrown out on impact. His mind was racing. He fought to regain control of his body. He managed to land on his hands and knees and rolled. His forward speed and the slight downward slope of the hill made each roll about thirty feet in length. He could see the chopper looming directly over him. The wounded bird made a terrible screeching and grinding noise, metal on rock. It completed its death sentence and seemed determined to take his life with it. From the corner of his eyes, he caught a glimpse of two trees during his second tumble. On his third roll he managed to kick up and go between the two trees, using them as a barrier from the chopper. It worked. The chopper skidded to a halt a short distance from him. His maneuver had saved his life. He didn't have time to congratulate himself. There was no ground on the other side of the trees. He fell almost twenty feet down the side of a steep ravine. He broke his ankle when he hit the ground.

Today just isn't your day, is it? He forced himself to an upright position. The initial shock of what he had just been through wore off quickly, and his thoughts turned to his team trapped inside the helicopter. Standing up sent a sickening nauseous taste through his mouth. He began to pull himself up the side of the ravine. Thoughts of getting to his team and pulling them out of the chopper before it exploded made him forget about his pain. As he scrambled to the top and hobbled towards the helicopter, fear came to him in waves. He was terrified of the chopper exploding and killing the men still trapped inside. He could hear voices yelling, "Smoke! Smoke!" He moved closer to the wounded bird.

He could hear the engine running. Now he had two fears tugging at him: one pushing him to get his team out, the other telling him to get away before the chopper exploded. He couldn't see out of his right eye; it was bleeding. His breathing was coming in shallow gasps, and each breath grew more painful. He knew his back was broken. For a brief second, he contemplated giving up. No one would blame him if he just lay down and let whatever was meant to happen, happen. He quickly shoved these cowardly thoughts aside, ashamed to have such things like this enter his mind. There was no way he could have lived knowing he had not done everything possible to save his team. He was less than ten feet from the chopper. He saw the senior medic hobbling towards him. He was either thrown or had jumped out on the other side of the helicopter. The two of them began throwing rucksacks and climbing gear out to get to the men buried underneath. The first one cleared of the tangled mess was the team leader. He didn't have a single scratch on him. With his help, they uncovered the remaining injured team members.

He opened the door of the Huey and grabbed the pilot. He unhooked his seat belt. The pilot regained consciousness just long enough to shut the engine off. The pilot's face had a deep cut running from the side of his cheekbone to his lower lip. His teeth were exposed in a sickening grin. It took two of them to get the pilot out. Once he was clear of the chopper the pilot regained total consciousness. He calmly walked up hill a few feet and hit his emergency radio frequency. A low-flying jet pinpointed their location, and in twenty minutes he was being placed onto a stretcher and hoisted onto another helicopter identical to the one lying on the ground. He relaxed as much as possible. He was being flown to the nearest German hospital. Sure hope this one doesn't crash, he thought.

He regained his senses as the chopper was setting down. He was wheeled into the emergency room where German doctors and nurses went to work on him. They took x-rays of his head, back, and ankles. The hospital staff went to work sewing up the large gash on his forehead.

The army chaplain broke the news of his injuries to his wife and son. He saw the look of shock on her face when she entered the room and saw him lying there, his head almost twice its normal size. He had a cast on his left foot which was propped up on pillows. He had numerous cuts, scratches, and bruises. She took a chair beside his bed and reached out tenderly to take his hand in hers. She didn't say anything. She sat praying, "Thank you, Lord."

Her words faded. He dozed off into a drug-induced sleep. A picture of the ground kept coming up as the chopper came crashing down. An instant replay of the crash played over and over in his dreams throughout the night.

His wife and son were there the day he was released from the hospital. He was fully dressed when they arrived. His stitches had been removed, and he had shaved. More than anything else he wanted a bath, but he would have to wait until he got home. His wife had to put his shoes on for him. He caught the look of despair that passed over his son's face and realized this was the first time the boy had seen his dad in such a weakened state. He looked away quickly so his son would not notice he was reading his thoughts. He felt his heart swell up with pride as he was being pushed by his son to their car.

"Don't worry, pops. We will take care of you for a change."

1984 For the past year, after the chopper crash, he tried to stay on the team. Although his back had healed, it was not satisfactory. He realized his days on an A-team were numbered. The three broken and compressed vertebrae would sap him of his strength under a large amount of stress, and the weight of his rucksack caused him excruciating pain.

He took his time through the summer doing what the doctors had ordered. He went to physical therapy and worked out cautiously at first. His running legs had returned. He could do a mile in less than five-and-a-half minutes and was up to five miles in under thirty-two minutes within three months. But he could tell he was not like he had been. After each parachute jump, he had to seek out a chiropractor and have his back realigned.

He had been recommended for the soldier's medal for his actions at the chopper crash, but it had been denied by his battalion commander. He had done what a Special Forces soldier was supposed to do. He would have been embarrassed had he received any medals for his action. He was extremely pissed off when the same award had been turned down for his senior medic. Years later, he would read in the *Army Times* newspaper of an officer getting the medal for doing the same thing. His senior medic was medically discharged for his injuries. Thanks to the medic's unselfish actions, everyone recovered. He had done what a Special Forces medic was supposed to do even though he did it with five broken vertebrae.

He was dreading his first winter warfare training exercise. His rucksack weighed over 130 pounds. Everything he needed for the six-week stay in the mountains to sustain him packed inside. His team members divided the team gear up. They gave him just a few batteries to carry. He insisted they also give him a 150-foot rope to carry, to which they reluctantly agreed. He sat inside the aircraft as he had done hundreds of times doing a quick calculation of his weight. His rucksack weighed 130 pounds, his main parachute was thirty-five pounds, his reserve was fifteen pounds, and ammo, canteens, and other miscellaneous items in his pockets were another fifteen pounds. He would exit the aircraft with equipment weighing over 195 pounds. He, himself, was up to 150 pounds.

It took two men to help him to his feet. One of them had to hook his static line in place for him since he couldn't reach above his head with the weight he carried. The bucking aircraft made it very difficult to maintain his balance. He knew if he fell he wouldn't be able to get up by himself either. The slow nagging fear that had become so much a part of his life returned. Would he be able to carry all of this equipment off the drop zone?

They made their exit from the big iron bird on time. Upon landing, he quickly disconnected his reserve and shook off his main chute. There was a flashlight coming in his direction. "Put that damn light out," he ordered. Whoever was walking around with the light was breaking all security operating procedures. Even though this was just a training mission, no lights ever came on unless there was a serious injury. The light was headed in his direction.

"That you, top?" It was his company commander, a major that he had the utmost respect for.

"Yeah, it's me." The major turned the light off and skied up to him.

"Sorry about the light, but I lost my Rolex while setting up this drop zone for you broke dicks." Dicks, that was his favorite word for all the teams in his company. He had just finished stowing the parachute inside the kit bag and securing the reserve to the top handles as his commander came up to him.

"Here, let me give you a hand with that," said the major and took the kit bag before he could protest. He headed off for the turn-in point. He quickly got his skis and ruck on and took out in the same direction. He knew his company commander did not own a Rolex.

Six weeks of skiing up and down the mountains in Germany, doing one mission after another to test the team's readiness, had taken its toll on everyone. Each man had lost at least ten to fifteen pounds. His shoulders had suffered the familiar bruises. The pain from his back kept him awake many nights in too much discomfort to sleep.

The temperatures dropped as low as sixty degrees below zero each night. The constant shivering placed a great deal of strain on his back, and it gave him hell day and night. He could barely help pitch a tent to sleep in after their long mountain treks.

He felt helpless with the amount of work the others had to do for him. This would be his last mission on an A-team. He was glad it was just a training mission. He knew his team held back a lot in order for him to keep up. The x-rays told the story. His back looked worse than a ninety-year-old man's. The doctor's exact words to him when he showed him the compressed vertebras and the loss of bone were that the x-rays revealed that his bones were actually starting to flare out. "How much weight do you carry on that back?" His doctor asked, awestruck.

He returned to his company headquarters. His wife held him that night and tried to reassure him life would go on even though he was no longer on an A-team. She knew his pride—the pride to strive to be the best in everything; the pride his father had instilled in him as a young boy to take nothing unless he earned it. He was half-white and half-Indian. Which part of him hurt the most? She wondered. He told her he was going to work in the lower section of Bad Tolz. She knew through rumors from the other wives that this was a classified section, an area where they supposedly maintained the atomic bombs that Special Forces had the opportunity to use in time of war. She had learned a long time ago that secrets did not remain secrets very long in the Army. Although he would not talk about his job or missions, there were plenty of wives that seemed to know what was going on.

He reported to his new job feeling a little bit better. As the new acting command sergeant major, he would be directly responsible for the newest and latest security measures that were about to be installed. After going over plans with the civilian contractors, he was satisfied with everything. That is, everything that had been planned. He wanted one item installed that the contractor had not been hired to create. He thought it was vital that an override system be implemented which would allow access to nuclear devices if all electrical power was lost, a likely event in the time of war. With his persuasion, an override system to the large internal steel doors was installed. Simple yet practical, the huge doors could be opened with a regular car battery. It allowed anyone with the proper code to enter and retrieve the nuclear weapons. He tested this system on a regular basis to ensure it was working properly. It worked perfectly each time. For the rest of his time in the Army, he worked with the security and care of nuclear weapons. He traveled extensively, inspecting and making recommendations to upgrade any lapses of security. He set up and implemented many standard operating procedures. He saw the accomplishment of the latest nuclear bombs made exclusively for Special Forces. His favorite was a small device that contained more power than both bombs dropped on Japan. It was light and resembled an ordinary business man's suitcase. This new device revolutionized the ability of Special Forces to get in and destroy a specific target. It was much smaller and lighter than anything in their arsenal.

Her parents were dead. They were killed in a car accident by a semi-tractor. The three of them flew home and took care of the funeral arrangements. He felt lost. There was nothing he could do to ease her grief. He and his son just stayed with her day and night, talking when she wanted to talk. He sat with her when she was in too much sorrow to speak, and he hugged her when she cried. It was a trying time for all of them. He was thankful they couldn't stay. He had to get back to Germany. He felt that it was the best thing for her, to go on living with the living. You have to keep on living.

She healed slowly from her loss. She thanked the two of them one night for being there for her. She did not know what she would have done without her two special men. They sat on the couch and held her for a long time. She had one final good cry and the next day was back to her old self. It was several more months before she could laugh wholly, like she used to. When he heard it some time later, he knew she was going to be alright.

CHAPTER 15

1994

Where had the years gone? They watched with pride as their son accepted his college degree and walked off the stage. They looked into each other's eyes. They didn't need words. They had done a good job. Before them stood a fine young man with character and dignity.

His son would pursue his dream of law enforcement. He wanted his son to become a lawyer, but he supported his decision wholeheartedly. His son's dream was to work for the FBI. They were going to spend the summer together hiking the Appalachian Trail, the three of them together. It was the end of May, and all the final preparations were packed in the van. They spent the morning having breakfast with the next-door neighbors. The old couple had become like family to them over the past five years. The old couple had stopped by the first evening they had moved into the house. The three of them had been tired after a long day of unpacking and moving furniture. He was sitting in his easy chair trying to relax his tired back muscles when there was a knock on the front door. His son had answered it. He heard him say, "Will you marry me?" Someone laughed, and the rest was muffled.

His son entered the living room with a pleasant-looking couple.

"Dad these are our neighbors who live in the first house down the road." He proceeded to make the introductions.

"We thought you might be hungry after all the work you've been doing," said the woman. She had a basket dangling from her hand. "I asked your son at the door if he liked fried chicken, and he proposed to me!" She spoke with laughter in her voice.

Her husband remarked with a twinkle in his blue eyes that there would have to be a duel of pistols for his woman. He had spent too many years eating her bad cooking. Now that she almost had it right he wasn't going to let her go without a fight. His wife's free arm poked him square in the ribs for his remark. Just like my wife, he thought. The five of them sat at the kitchen table and dove into the best fried chicken he'd ever had. The old man had retired five years earlier from the railroad. They had been married for almost forty-five years. They did not have any children due to the old man's childhood disease. By the time they stopped talking, it was past midnight. His son had compromised with the old man on his marriage proposal. As they walked them down the driveway his son said, "I'll let you keep your wife if you are willing to adopt me. I'm short a grandma and grandpa."

The old woman stopped walking and put her arms around him. She gave him a warm hug. "Look no further," she replied. The old couple had quickly become a part of their lives. The old man loved to fish, something he had never had the patience for. His son, however, was an avid fisherman. The old man and his son spent a lot of time on the riverbank just a mile down the road. Since he didn't like fishing, he was voted the cook. They spent many pleasant summer nights on the patio with the smell of fresh fish on the grill.

The old couple walked them to the van, and hugs were given all around. "Grandma," as his son called her, wiped the tears from her eyes. She gave them all a scolding for going so far away and being gone for a month. The old man assured him they would keep an eye on the house and collect the mail. A final hug, and the old couple waved as they drove away. They were finally on the road to trek the Appalachian Trail.

There was no time schedule. They began their hike in Georgia and would walk for thirty days, camping out under the stars at night. Each of them carried a backpack with a sleeping bag and several changes of clothing. The food, stove, first aid kit, rope and climbing gear were distributed evenly between the three of them. All three of them were in good physical shape. The walk through the mountains was easy and relaxing.

The days quickly passed. They shared the picturesque country, stopping to appreciate the view. At night they sat by the campfire, talking and telling stories. The glow flickered a dusky yellow on his son's and wife's faces. He looked at both of them, and his heart filled with pride. His wife looked so happy. She was so full of life. She looked at him, and her eyes were filled with adoration for both her boys.

"Thank you, Lord," he had whispered under his breath. He was so grateful to have them in his life.

Towards the middle of their hike one night, his son asked him, "When do you plan on retiring?"

After giving it some thought he said, "I think another three years is all I can handle."

"What will you and mom do then?" His son said with a mouthful of peanut butter sandwich.

"I would like to take your lovely mother and travel through every state in the union. Now that you are moving out, we no doubt will have plenty of money. The savings on the food bill alone should pay for a small recreational vehicle and several new cars!"

His son laughed, "I'm not out of the house yet. So don't go counting your spare change too quickly." The month passed too quickly for all of them. They were sitting around their last campfire and for some reason he felt the need to share with them his Indian heritage. They stayed up through the night as he told stories of his mother's family.

His mother had been born on the reservation that bordered his father's land. There was slightly under a thousand acres that many men had tried to steal over the past 200 years. It was still in the family. He told his son that one day the land would be his. He must promise to never sell it. His ancestors lived there in a deep sleep. There may come a time when future generations would have need of a sanctuary, a place to survive in a time of trouble. He spoke long into the night relaying stories his father had told him as a boy about his mother and the rich history of the Indian nations. He told them of the wood spirits on his land and how they used to play with him as a young boy. If you listen they will tell you what you need to know, where the deer are resting, which way to go, how to find water, he said. Many things live in the forest you must find and see for yourself someday.

He veered off and told them stories of his childhood—the fights in school, the way people made fun of his beliefs, and the hardships of poverty. He found himself telling them all about his beautiful mother and the sister he never knew. He went on a long time about his mother and father and how he missed them. He even shared the innermost secrets of his dreams and how his mother would appear to him. He talked on and on for several hours, sharing his pain with the only two people who could begin to understand. Finally it grew quiet and without a word both of them held him as though their love could erase his pain. It didn't, but it helped him more than they would ever know.

1995

His time in the Army was growing short. He looked forward to retirement with mixed emotions. He peeked in on his wife and saw that she was still sleeping. He was in the process of making her breakfast, a habit he got into when he was home.

It was a Saturday morning, and he wanted to surprise her. As he entered their bedroom he could not help but smile. How magnificent she looked. She had not changed in all these years. She had some lines around her eyes and her weight had increased slightly, but he saw none of this. In his mind she had remained the same attractive woman he watched sleeping on his chest all those years before. He set the tray of food on the bedstand, then leaned over and gave her a kiss on the cheek. He growled like a bear, and he chewed lightly on her ear. She stirred and opened her eyes. He brushed her hair from her face and kissed her lightly on the lips.

"Good morning, handsome," she grinned. "What have you been up to?"

"Why, I've been slaving away in the kitchen for the last hour making the most beautiful woman in the world a breakfast fit for a princess." He hoped she wouldn't notice the slightly overdone toast on the tray. "Is there any thing else the lady requires?" She held out her arms and pulled him to her for another kiss. The blankets fell and gave him a glimpse of her breast. He felt the familiar stirring; she whispered what she wanted. Well, we will just have to microwave those omelets and potatoes later, he thought.

He woke up, and the rain was pouring down in a cloud burst. His retirement ceremony would have to take place inside the auditorium rather than on the parade field. Good, no need to have all the soldiers standing in formation as he was recognized for his years of service.

The band played several marching songs while he was led up on stage. He was given this honor. As the group commander read off his list of achievements and military awards, he stood staring at his wife who sat in the seat beside him.

"Thank you," he said to her just loud enough for her to hear.

Teary-eyed she said, "Thank you."

His son sat in the front row, and he could see his face beam with pride. He couldn't look at him for fear of choking up. His farewell speech was short: thirty years in the best Army in the world, working with the best soldiers in the world. Now it was time for him to leave. He recalled several funny stories where he was in trouble and the lessons he learned from them. He thanked everyone for being there, and it was over.

The night before he had dreamed of his mother: she had been crying. Her troubled face came to him just as he was finishing his farewell speech, and he glanced at his wife.

Now, he was a civilian, the most dreaded term for anyone who is a career soldier. They drove through the rain to their favorite restaurant for a late afternoon lunch. His son told them of his latest job assignments in the FBI. He had nothing good to say about the current administration in the White House, and how frustrated he was with all the red tape and lack of funds to operate in a productive manner. He could only chuckle and respond with, "At least you did not have to serve under Jimmy."

After dinner, they drove home. The rain had slowed to a slight mist. He drove the car up to their house. He saw a large motor home parked in the driveway.

"Wonder who that could be?" He was slightly miffed that the large beast was taking up all the driveway space. Now he was forced to drive on the grass to get around it. He caught a look of delight pass over his son's eyes. The boy never could play poker. He played along for his son's sake. He went up to the RV and knocked on the door. He stood there with his wife, "Are we expecting any visitors?" His son quietly moved between them and placed his arms around them. He chuckled,

"Happy retirement, folks. Hope you like your new traveling companion."

Her last day of work! She drove to the hospital thinking how good it would be to sleep in with her husband. The RV was packed, ready and waiting. They would spend a few days at home making a few last minute preparations and then it was off to circumvent the entire United States. She felt a warm glow when she thought of her son's generous gift to them. He was a great kid. One of their first stops would be a visit with their son in D.C. for several weeks. She pulled into the quick mart for her usual morning cup of coffee and paper. She didn't see the car coming down the street or the drunk driver swerving side to side. She walked around the back of her car. She heard someone yell, "Look out!" She looked up in time to see the driver's face. His car slammed into her. His eyes never even blinked. The impact crushed her hips and vertebrae. She was pinned between the two cars.

The driver got out of the car and casually walked away. He didn't even look back. The paramedics who arrived on the scene knew her. They had worked with her in the hospital for the past ten years. If they hadn't been called out on this emergency, they would still be at the hospital with the rest of the staff, waiting for her to come in so they could give her a surprise retirement party. The ambulance crew had been responsible for getting the balloons and decorations. The EMTs were well-trained. They moved like choreography. Their actions were smooth and efficient within the small compartment of the ambulance. Despite their best efforts to save her, she died en route to the hospital.

CHAPTER 17

It was a clear day, the kind of day that made you feel alive. The sun was busy playing a child's game of peek-a-boo through snowy white clouds. This was not the kind of day to bury the woman you loved. She should be here with you, enjoying a day like this. She would have mentioned the elegant cotton clouds against the turquoise sky. She would have laughed and made sweet music.

The service was over. All the friends and relatives had long departed, leaving only the two men standing beside her grave with their grief. unable to speak or move. They couldn't find the strength to leave her. It was all they could do to find the will to breathe. Each one was wrapped in private precious memories too painful to bear, yet unable to stop. They stood there together, the younger of the two a good head taller than the older man, neither aware of the sun as it dipped lower and lower in the sky. They stood silently beside the grave, as the burial detail covered her with the dirt. Lord, I would've given anything for that grave not to have been dug in the first place. Why her? Why didn't you take me? His son's sobs broke his heart all the more. Somewhere in the past a lone warrior had stood over his bride and felt the pain he was feeling now. A low moan escaped his lips. The image floated through his being.

They stayed by the gravesite until darkness drove them to their home. Neighbors and friends were waiting for them. They took turns bringing in food and cards of sympathy. Each of them felt sorry for the two men. They couldn't bring themselves to talk, only nod and shake their hands. There was nothing they could do to relieve their pain. All of them searched for ways to try, knowing it impossible.

The day came when he had to report back to work. He had stayed home with his dad for two weeks. He wanted to stay longer, but his dad insisted that he leave. His friends at the FBI had told him to take as much time as he needed. They would cover his caseload until he came back to work. His dad walked him to his car. They hugged each other, one feeling the loss as deeply in the other. No words were necessary, just a hug and a wave goodbye. He felt even worse as he realized how small and how much older his father looked in that last moment as he drove away.

The house was empty now. He sat watching the nightly news but took little interest in the latest White House scandal. He had been a soldier and had allowed politicians to send him around the world, doing what they thought was best for America. He couldn't understand how an obvious draft dodger during the Vietnam War could become president. Even more confusing to him was the number of World War II veterans that supported him. He turned the television off and headed slowly to the bedroom. He stood looking at her favorite picture of the three of them, high on the Appalachian Trail with the mountains above and the river running below them. A lone hiker had been kind enough to happen by and take the photograph for them. He ran his finger over her face. Then, as he had done every night for the past six months, he said her name out loud softly and wept. His shoulders finally sagged from a weight he could not carry.

CHAPTER 18

Today was court day. The man who had murdered his wife was to be sentenced. He had to be there. He had to see the court system work. He needed to look his wife's killer in the face when he received his just punishment. His son wanted to be there, but his job required him to testify in another state. He shaved and put on his new suit, the one he had purchased for this very day. The life insurance company had sent him a check for one hundred thousand dollars. He had used the money to buy the suit. He had not spent a single penny of it for anything else. He had been there every day during the trial. He sat in the back observing his wife's killer, a big slob who was over six-foot-four, weighing over 240 pounds. Even with his hair cut and a new set of clothes, he looked dirty and unkept.

He heard the defense attorney tell the jury how this young man was a product of today's modern society; how he had been a latch key kid with no parental support; how his mother had six kids by several different boyfriends; how he had been bullied in school and forced to drop out for being poor. How could this young man find a job with his lack of education? Because of his miserable lifestyle with no hope of a bright future, society forced him into a life of drugs and escape from his everyday troubles.

"Your honor, my client is very remorseful for the tragic accident that took a life. He has entered into a drug rehabilitation program. He is now trying to obtain his high school GED. Although the loss of life is unforgivable, I believe my client has been made a better person by this experience. His recent behavior testifies to his sincere efforts to change and become a productive member of society. He deserves another chance. Let's give him that chance now. Don't place this young man in a prison full of convicts. Don't deny him his one chance to change, now that he has seen a better life is possible. He's like a drowning man: we can give him a rope that will save him or toss him a stone to take him under forever."

The killer maintained a stony face throughout the trial. He didn't look at the jury or at his surroundings. He was sure the killer knew who he was. The killer's lawyer had pointed him out the first day of the court proceedings. He arrived at the courthouse early and waited in the hallway until he was ushered in by a police officer. He took his usual seat in the back of the courtroom. The judge came in, and every one stood in honor of his position before taking their seats again.

The jury had found the killer guilty. The jury had wanted to see him held accountable for his actions. Today the judge would pronounce his sentence. The judge had the killer stand, and he gave a lengthy monologue of the killer's need to reform and the consequences he would face in prison if he did not. The judge found him guilty of involuntary manslaughter, gave the killer five years probation, suspended his license for three years, and ordered him to perform one hundred hours of community service. There was some clamor as a number of surprised voices objected to this unreasonably light verdict. He didn't hear them. The shock of knowing his wife's killer was going to go free, not going to jail for a long time, took the wind out of him.

The courtroom cleared after the judge had pronounced a five-year probation and time served. He remained in his chair watching the punk receive congratulations from his friends. His lawyer beamed with pride. He was still sitting there as the killer and his friends walked past him.

The bastard couldn't help himself. Perhaps it was his bad upbringing, or maybe he just wanted to look tough in front of his friends. Whatever the reason, it was a grave mistake. He stopped in front of the little man sitting there and said in a loud voice, "Man, I sure wish I could have fucked her before she died. That looked like one great piece of ass."

There was a sudden stillness as even his friends were shocked from his remark. He stood with a smirk on his face. He glanced around at his friends looking for approval for his bad ass remark.

The man sitting in the chair slowly turned his eyes towards his wife's killer and locked eyes with him. The juvenile lost his smile and for the first time in his life he saw death. He saw true naked death staring in his face. The green, smoldering eyes locked onto his and went to the very depth of his soul. A cold chill went through him. He was suddenly very much afraid of this man. Something tugged in the back recess of his mind. He had just made the biggest mistake of his life. After leaving the courthouse with his friends, he remained boisterous and loud. But he couldn't shake off the uneasy feeling. He finally convinced himself that it was his imagination. Besides this was not the time to think of that little old fucker. He was way overdue on getting high and getting laid. Shoving his friend out of the way he got behind the wheel of the car and spun out of the parking lot. He drove on the wrong side of the road taking large sips from a bottle of whiskey.

Still, for several months after the trial he could not fall asleep with out seeing those eyes, the eyes of death that penetrated into the very depths of his soul.

Where was he? The thoughts filtered intermittently into his brain. He had been at a party with his old running buddies. They had a great time with a fifteen-year-old girl. Each of them had taken turns with her as she lay passed out on the floor. His head hurt from too much booze and dope. For some reason he could not move. His eyes finally focused, and he looked around. He was somewhere in a forest. The fog began to dissipate from his mind. Something was definitely wrong. He felt sick. When he tried to move, he discovered he was tied up. He began to put the pieces of the previous night together. They had all partied long into the night. Most of his friends had fallen asleep or passed out on the living room floor. All except him. He waited for the young girl to pass out again after giving her a large glass of brandy laced with a small amount of cocaine. He had carried her to the bedroom where he intended to fulfill a few sadistic fantasies.

As he threw her on the bed, a hand had reached around his mouth. Thinking it was one of his friends, he started to say something. He must have blacked out,because he couldn't remember anything else. How did he get here? Why was he tied up? If this was a sick joke, he was going to kick some serious ass. He heard a slight rustling in the trees. Standing before him was the little man. How did he get so close without being seen? How had he managed to carry him to such a remote spot in the forest? He couldn't see any roads or vehicles.

The little man had allowed his hair to grow. He had tied a bandana around his head to keep the hair out of his eyes. What had it been now? Over a year since he had last seen him in the courtroom. Time enough to have pushed him from his mind. Time enough so that he quit looking over his shoulder expecting to see him. The killer decided that if he ever did run into this little fuck, he was going to beat him within an inch of his life. And now here he was, bound tightly to a small tree looking at the past. He didn't like the sinking feeling that was creeping slowly upward from his belly to settle around his chest. It was difficult for him to breathe. The little man slid a backpack from his shoulders. He watched the little guy take a small tent from the pack and put it together. He hung the pack on a tree limb. Then he took out a sheet of paper from the backpack. He took out a stapler and a small wooden stick that had been sharpened on one end.

"What do you want, you little fuck?" his voice faltered. The man said nothing. He took the paper and stapled it to the small stick. He then walked slowly towards him and stuck the stick in the ground in front of him. He moved away in slow methodical steps. He saw that it was a picture that stapled to the stick. a picture of the woman that had been killed almost two years ago by his reckless driving. It was the little man's wife. The kid was scared shitless. He was able to bluff most of the time because of his size, but this time it was different. He knew he was going to die, and that it would be a very long time before death would release him. He knew the last thing he would ever see on this earth was that picture. He started to cry. He pissed involuntarily.

How long had it been? Four days or four weeks? The pain was unbearable. There was a small fire to illuminate the darkness that surrounded him. First, his jaw was broken. Surprising, the little man did not use a club or baseball bat. He tried to bluff the little bastard by threatening to kick his ass when he got loose from the ropes. He spat at the picture in front of him and demanded to be released. The man had casually walked by and kicked him. When he finally came to his senses, he couldn't talk. His jowl hung to the left side of his face at an impossible angle. His head had been tied to the tree so he was only able to stare at the picture of the woman. He had spent two days in this position, working at the ropes that bound him, his head pounding with every heartbeat.

Water was given to him twice a day—not from kindness, he knew, but to keep him alive. One sip in the morning and one again in the evening. The third day his feet were crushed and his elbows broken with the aid of a small hammer. The blows smashed his ankles with one exact stroke on each foot. The elbows were even more painful. A precise blow to the very tip of the bone smashed the fragments deep into his useless arms. With his broken jaw stuffed with an old rag, all he could manage was a gurgling whimper, not loud enough for anyone to hear, had there been anyone to hear. Time was not measured in seconds or minutes any longer, but rather by each beat of his heart. This morning he had been scalped. The knife flashed so quickly above his head. Only when he felt a powerful tug and heard the sickening pop that followed did he realize what was happening to him. Despite his broken jaw, he let out a blood curdling squeal.

He had tried to refuse water, to allow death to come more quickly. But he lacked the self-discipline. Each time he was offered the warm liquid, he greedily drank all of it and would have begged for more if he could have spoken. He couldn't keep his eyes closed for very long. A glowing stick from the fire was held against his groin until he opened his eyes. His testicles had suffered the most from the hot stick. They were now just blackened chards of melting flesh. As long as he sat and stared at the picture he was left alone until evening.

He had the timetable worked out now. Sleep after torture for a few hours, water, and then he sat staring at the picture until dusk. Then he would sleep for several more hours before he was awakened and forced to look at the picture until sunrise, water. He waited in terror for the sun to set. Tonight, the first joint of every finger and toe had been cut off and thrown into the fire. He could see and smell his own flesh burning. His scalp had been stuck on a pole outside the tent. He watched it ooze drops of blood throughout the day. The flies had swarmed around him. There was a bandana tied around his head to keep the blood from blocking his view of that dreaded picture. His hands and feet bled very little because the ropes were bound so tightly that they cut off most of the circulation. Somewhere in the back of his mind he knew his time was about up. No human could under go this amount of torture and live very long. He could see the small red streaks creeping up his legs where the bones had been shattered. He imagined his arms looked the same. Tomorrow he would refuse the water. He would show that son of a bitch that he would control his own death. To hell with him.

Morning came bringing with it a new hunger for life. He was waiting for the cup of water. He needed it so badly. Where was his water? Nothing else mattered now but getting his water. The little man had not appeared like he always did. Had he left him? The tent was no longer there, neither was the rucksack. The only thing that remained was the picture. It was just inches from his face. Was he being left alone to die? A new fear came over him. Was he being left for the animals to eat alive? Were there any bears in this forest? Where the hell was that son of a bitch? He didn't have to wait long for the answers. He closed his eyes for a few seconds. When he opened them the little man was standing before him. He took out his knife and with a few strokes cut his bonds. Before he knew what was happening, he was picked up and thrown over a shoulder. How can someone so small carry me like I'm nothing? The journey was several hundred yards but seemed a lifetime. Each step his tormentor took brought forth wave after wave of agony. He was thrown on the ground and tied again.

This time his legs were crossed and bound in front of him. His hands were tied to his legs. He managed a slight whimper. His head was jerked back sharply, and his eyelids were stitched with a needle and thread so that he couldn't blink. The needle felt a little more to him than a mosquito bite. Another rope was secured around and under his armpits. The rope was thrown over a tree limb and he was pulled to about four feet from the ground. He was left to swing for awhile. Was he going to be left to die in this position? His vision blurred and the little man appeared before him with the same picture and something new. He carried a three-foot wooden stick that had been sharpened on both ends. The picture was placed in front of him and the long stick was stuck into the ground directly beneath him. Suddenly he realized he would die today. He was going to be lowered over the sharp stick that was placed directly beneath his asshole. He was crying now and mad. He was not even going to get his usual cup of water.

He was dying. Soon his blackened soul would leave his tortured body. The stick had penetrated him. It went up his rectum as he was lowered by the rope. Nothing he had experienced up to this point came close to this. He felt the splintery wood rip at his insides. He couldn't pass out. He could not scream. All he could muster was a continuous grunt. Somehow the stick had missed his heart. It protruded from his back just below his shoulder blade. The picture was now being held by his tormenter inches from his face. He saw nothing but the picture through the haze of blood still seeping from the stitches. He knew the man would stand there, holding it until the end came. God, he pleaded, please make it quick. But God was not listening to him. He lived until sunset, staring at the woman he had killed.

CHAPTER 19

He awoke with a splitting headache made worse by the constant banging of what remained of the awning. The wind had torn it off the RV six months earlier, leaving the top metal casing for the wind to catch and sling against the side of the RV repeatedly. The noise was so loud it had awakened him many times in the past weeks from a drunken sleep. He was somewhere in New Mexico. He had driven that far before he was forced to stop out of sheer exhaustion. He was parked on national forest land, far enough off the road so he wouldn't be noticed or bothered by the passing traffic but close enough to a small country store where he could walk whenever the whiskey ran out.

He made a weekly trip to the country store. He filled a small backpack with as many bottles of whiskey as it would hold. Sometimes he grabbed cans of food off the shelf without looking or caring to see what the contents were. For the past five months, he had been living here, drinking until he would pass out, only to awaken and drink some more. Food was something that his body would demand on occasion. He would eat whatever he pulled from the cupboard, directly from the can. After he ate as much as his stomach would take, he tossed the can and the remaining contents out the window. A large stockpile of empty cans and whiskey bottles now stared back at him. Wild animals would come around during the night and take care of any remaining food.

He forced himself not to think. When his tormented mind wondered too far into the past, he would drink. His beard and hair were long and dirty. His water reserves in the RV had been empty for over three months. He could have driven to the store and filled his tanks with fresh water, but he chose not to.

When his water had run out, he had simply quit bathing. His body was filthy from the sand and months of improper hygiene. A jug of bottled water sat on the counter. He had not touched it since he purchased it over a month ago.

His head would not stop hurting. The wind would not stop blowing. The awning cover, for some reason, reminded him of a Chinese water torture; it continued to hit the side of the RV. The noise was loud and irregular like the wind. A sudden gust picked up, bringing with it more fine sand through the window he had neglected to close. His nose was full of the fine misty particles. He needed to flush out his nose, get rid of the sand. Maybe it would ease the pain in his head. Slowly getting up from the couch, he shut the window. He picked up the bottle of cheap whiskey and took a long swallow. His belly lurched as the warm liquid burned the lining of his stomach. He picked up the bottle of water and poured some into a plastic pan. He tilted the pan and placed his nostrils in the water and sucked the water up his nose. He gagged as the water came down the back of his throat. It sent the contents of his stomach up his throat and onto the floor.

He was down to his last bottle of whiskey. He knew it was time to make his weekly trip to the store for more. He picked up his backpack and staggered out the door. A gust of wind slammed the awning cover above his head sending a sharp pain through his head. His tortured mind snapped completely. Instead of heading in the direction of the highway, he started walking into the desert. It was time for him to die. Time to end the pain, the constant pain of loss that time had failed to erase.

Where was his dad? The question had been on his mind for the past several months. At first he thought dad was just driving around the country healing his broken heart in his own way. He called the house and got the answering machine. He wasn't suspicious. After the third call uneasiness began to creep into his thoughts. The neighbors had not seen or heard from him. They were keeping the house under watch and promised to call him if they saw or heard from him.

There was probably nothing to worry about. The RV was gone. Maybe he felt the need to get away and drive around the country like he and mom had planned. Still he felt uneasy. This was not like his dad. He always kept in touch. He drove from his Washington, D.C., apartment to their old house outside of Fort Bragg. The car was parked in the driveway. The grass was in need of cutting. The mailbox was empty. There were no visible signs of a forced entry or burglary. He went into the house. Nothing was out of place or out of the ordinary. His father always was a neat freak. He smiled. The memories floated through his mind of the happy times he had in this home, the practical jokes the three of them used to play on each other. A knocking on the front door interrupted his thoughts. His neighbor stood there holding a box of mail and newspapers.

"I'm so glad to see you," she spoke through a worried smile. "I've been collecting your dad's mail for him."

"Hi, grandma," he squeezed her gently.

"He never said anything to anyone, just drove off in the RV one afternoon. We have been so worried. Why hasn't he called?"

He thanked her for her help and after a few pleasantries she left, knowing he needed to be alone. He went to the phone and listened to the numerous messages. Besides his, there were several from his dad's old Army buddies. Nothing to indicate where his dad was off to. He left a note on the kitchen table in case his dad should return. After calling and canceling the local newspaper, he locked the door and drove to the post office. There, he had all mail transferred to his address in Washington, D.C. There was nothing more he could do. He wearily headed back to Washington with a feeling of uneasiness creeping up on him. Something was wrong.

It took three weeks before the first lead on his father's whereabouts surfaced. A credit card statement indicated that a purchase had been made at a small convenience store in New Mexico. Relief swept through him and brought tears to his eyes. His dad was probably just traveling around the country like he planned.

He was concerned with the items purchased though. The list was mainly whiskey, and lots of it. Several cans of food were also charged. As far as he knew, his dad had never taken another drink since his bachelor's party. He remembered the story his mother had told him about that party. His dad sat in stony silence when the two of them laughed hysterically. He missed him. He missed her too.

After receiving the next statement with almost the exact same contents, he knew his dad was in trouble. It was time for action on his part. He explained his thoughts and fears to his supervisor. Using vacation time, he took the next flight out of D.C. to Albuquerque, New Mexico. He leased a rental car and drove towards Gallup. He took the exit where the country store was located. A young Navaho Indian girl was working the cash register. She seemed shy and unwilling to answer his questions concerning the man whose picture he held before her. Then he explained to her, the man he was looking for was his father. He showed her another picture of his dad with him and his own identification. It seemed to relax her.

"The man in the picture could be the strange guy that came into the store every Tuesday. But the guy had longer hair and a beard. And," she said, almost embarrassed, "he is very dirty."

"Do you know where he lives?"

"No. He walks from that direction," she pointed, indicating the direction he had just came.

"Thank you." He drove into Gallup and got a room for the night. Today was Sunday. He would spend tomorrow searching for the RV. If that should fail, he would wait the following day at the convenience store. He went to sleep. He felt hopeful for the first time in months.

He took time to eat breakfast at a restaurant near his motel. The waitress gave him directions to the surrounding roads and RV parks. There were only two that she was aware of. One park was at the far end of town, and the other was just five miles down the road. It was a place called Red Rock State Park. He left the restaurant and turned right. He dismissed the other RV park. It was in the wrong direction and twenty miles from the liquor store his dad frequented. He drove slowly through the park. His heart sunk when he didn't find the RV. There was a small store in the park; "Trading Post" was burned into the wood above the door.

He spoke with a pleasant man and his wife who ran the store while he enjoyed a free cup of coffee. The couple's upbeat personalities and vast knowledge of the surrounding area was invaluable to him. After drawing him a sketch of the other more remote campsites located on national forest lands, the couple wished him luck. Shaking hands and taking a second cup of coffee at their insistence, he thanked them for their help. They followed him outside and stood there waving as he left the park. "Very nice people," he said to himself.

He pulled out of the park onto the main road. He saw an old Indian walking along the side of the road with his thumb out. The old man was wearing blue jeans and a fancy cowboy shirt. His head was covered with a weather-worn cowboy hat. He was going in the same direction, so he motioned for the old man to get in.

"Where are you headed?"

"I go to a little store just down the road," the old man replied. "It's not very far. Are you on vacation?"

"No, I'm looking for my father. Have you seen this man?" he said as he showed him a picture of his dad.

"I see him at the store where I go sometimes." For the first time he looked the old Indian directly in the eyes. He felt a slight chill pass through him. The old man's eyes had a warm look about them. They seemed familiar to him.

"I've only seen him once or twice." Then after a long pause he added, "He is sick man."

"Why do you say that?" His heart beat a little faster.

"Your father is sick in here." He pointed to his chest. "And he's sick here," pointing to his head. They drove the rest of the way in silence. They arrived at the country store, and the two of them walked inside. The old Indian paid for his tobacco. He asked about his father. The young girl had not seen him today.

"He is usually here by now," she said. He walked outside and nodded to the old men. Several nodded in return; most did not acknowledge him at all, treating him as though he was not there.

He got in his car and was about to place the keys in the ignition when the old Indian hitchhiker got back into his car. The old man just sat there in silence and after a few minutes he said, "Drive. I will help you find your father." He pulled out onto the road, and the old man pointed in the opposite direction of the camping areas.

"Your father not there; he wants to be alone. Go that way," he pointed east. He took the direction suggested by the old man. He turned back onto Interstate 40. After about five miles, the old man told him to get off at the next exit. He got off the main road and drove about a mile. The old man pointed to a trail that was barely visible. He took it. He began to wonder if the old man knew exactly where his father was. The road made a sharp curve behind some juniper trees, and there was the RV. It was completely hidden from the main road. He walked up to the RV. The two of them were assaulted with a sickening odor. They went inside and found the place was deserted. He could hardly breathe. The stench was coming from old vomit on the floor and the sewer tanks that were close to overflowing. Flies buzzed around and crawled over a decaying can of half-eaten meat. Maggots spilled from the can. The unsightly scene sent an alarm through him. His dad would never live in these conditions, at least, not in his right mind. He searched all the rooms, but no one was there. He went outside and looked at the pile of empty cans and broken whiskey bottles. While he had been waiting for his father to contact him, his dad had been living in his grief. He turned around and saw the old Indian standing beside the RV. He held a plastic jug of water he had taken from inside.

"We go that way," he said pointing southeast across a vast plain of sand. "Your father goes that way eight maybe more days ago."

"Why would he do that?"

"Your dad goes there to die." Coldness came over him.

"Shouldn't we go back to the store and phone the police and get a search party to help look?"

"No time." The old man said over his shoulder. He took off walking at a fast gait.

CHAPTER 20

Finishing the last drop of whiskey, he let the bottle drop from his hand and continued to walk, his eyes fixed on the horizon. He moved in slow methodical steps through the sand like he had been trained to do many years before. The boots he wore were ideal for this type of terrain. The dirty blue jeans and shirt he wore were not. In a short period of time he began to sweat from his exertions. The sun burned the top of his head. He didn't have a hat. His thin hair offered him no protection. The sweat that formed on his belly and chest ran downward inside his blue jeans. The moisture chafed his groin with each step. He had walked about six miles in the relentless sun when he came upon a small tree. The shade was not enough to offer him much relief from the heat, but it was enough to cover his head for a while. He lay down and slept.

He awoke just as the sun was about to set. He was thirsty. He wanted whiskey. He resisted the urge to walk back to the RV. The temperature was dropping fast. The sun had deserted him. With his hands he dug a small hole in the sand the length of his body and laid down. This would be as far as he would go. He would die here and be reunited with her.

He could feel her presence. The stars came out, and he talked to her for a long time. He told her how sorry he was that they couldn't finish their life together. He wept when he told her what he had done to her killer. It didn't make him feel any better, just all the more empty inside and alone. He missed her. He said it over and over again. His broken, lonely soul craved for her nearness. He begged God for hope, hope that he would not see tomorrow. He looked up at the moon, a moon he would regret seeing the next night if his prayer went unanswered. His thoughts whirled softly, and he fell asleep. He slept through the cold night dreaming of an old Indian man with kind eyes. They looked exactly like his mother's.

The first several days he almost gave up his desire to die. The need for whisky was so powerful, it overtook his every waking moment. He sat under a small tree baking under the torturous sun. He shook uncontrollably. His body demanded more alcohol. He didn't feel the need for water until the third day. The fifth day was the hardest; hunger crept into the recesses of his consciousness.

Demons came to him now, ghastly creatures of unspeakable horror. They showed him what the depths of hell looked like and how his soul would be tormented. They were around him day and night. They made fun of him and cursed him. He screamed when one demon grabbed his balls and ripped them off. Then the demon stood there in front of him eating them, and the blood ran down his long, boney fingers. The evil emanating from the eyes of his tormenter terrified him. Another demon took delight in stabbing its long pointed fingers into his stomach and pulling out his intestines before sucking them down his throat like spaghetti. He could see the reflection of his ashen face in the dark, sinister eyes of the monster before him. There were other demons floating about him. Several were holding pictures of his wife. Others told him he would soon join her in hell. Flashing before him in waves of blue light were images of his wife being raped by her murderer, and then the same man raping his mother. They begged him to help them. Their looks of fear and pain turned to ones of lust. They were now floating suspended in mid-air. Their legs were spread open wide. The soles of their feet were touching as they floated three feet off the ground. Their eyes became globes of evil delight. They took turns with his wife's killer. The murderer was standing in the middle of his mother and wife, thrusting at one and then turning to thrust at the other. There was a wooden stake protruding from his back. All eyes were casting evil glances at him. He heard himself screaming, "No! No!" until he was hoarse and couldn't utter another sound. He sobbed like a baby. "God help me. Please God!" He gave in to a deep, exhausted sleep.

The midday sun was throwing its furnace onto his blistered face. He couldn't move now. He was too weak from hunger and thirst. The sun had scorched his face over the past ten days. His face was covered with blisters. His tongue was too large for his mouth, and he could no longer swallow. Today or tomorrow he should die. He lost track of time, but he knew he should have died by now.

He had dreamed of the old Indian again, the one with the kind eyes. Eyes that looked so much like his mother's. Maybe I will meet you after I am dead. There was no longer any pain. He felt nothing. His kidneys had started to shut down. His mind raced with thoughts and questions. He felt at peace with himself. The heat and the cold did not seem to bother him anymore. His body was dehydrated beyond anything he had forced it to endure during his Special Forces days. He could no longer lift his arms or turn over. He was in a coma-like state, seeing his wife, his mother, his father. The three of them were standing under a large oak tree. It looked familiar to him, but for some reason he couldn't place it. There were rolling hills with snow-capped mountains under a brilliant Roman sky. They were beckoning to him. The three of them were smiling and were anxious that he should join them. His eyes were sore from the sight of them. How badly he needed to hug each of them. His dad seemed younger. His mother looked the same as he remembered her. His wife looked more dazzling than he had seen her before. She was jumping up and down, holding her arms out to him. He was running now. He took long, floating strides. His body moved effortlessly over the desert floor. He ran faster, pushing his muscles to exceed the blinding speed. Faster. His feet were no longer touching the ground. There was a tunnel of light. He was swept up by it, carried closer and closer to them. He was almost there. His wife couldn't wait anymore. She broke away from his parents and sprinted down the road to meet him. She looked so full of life just as he remembered her, the strawberry blonde hair flowing behind her as she ran towards him. Her white gown pressed against her body, and her voice called out to him. Suddenly she stopped running. Her eyes fell, her smile faded, she was still. Her arms dropped to her side. He struggled to move forward, to get to her, but some unseen force was pulling him back. He cried out her name and struggled with all his might to escape. She stood there, tears in her eyes. He heard her, and she was so close. But she was moving further away with each word.

"It's not time yet. You have to go back! Take care of our son. He needs you." Warm water ran down his throat, choking him. It brought him back to semi-consciousness. His life surged painfully through him once more. Someone was standing over him, shading him from the sun. He thought he heard his son's voice. More water was dribbled down his throat. Rough hands rubbed his face with water and cream. Slowly, against his will he opened his eyes to look upon the face of an old Indian man, the one he had seen in his dreams, the one with the kind eyes.

"I've seen you before," he whispered. The old man merely nodded and gave him another sip of water.

CHAPTER 21

His dad was dozing in the passenger seat. He slowed down, driving through the congested traffic of Oklahoma City. He would take his time getting back to D.C. He realized that he needed to spend as much time with his dad as possible. He glanced sideways at his father. He was awake and lighting up a cigarette. He had found a carton of Raleighs that had been packed by his mother. He found them cleaning the RV and getting it ready for the road trip. He had several days of hard work doing this while his dad recuperated in the hospital.

The old Indian had helped him carry his dad to the car. The old man insisted on sitting in the back with his father. He could see in the rear view mirror how the Indian held his father's head in an almost loving embrace. He gave him frequent sips of water while directing him to the hospital in Gallup.

During the confusing time of admitting his father into the hospital, filling out the insurance forms, and answering the police officer's questions, he had lost track of the old Indian. With regret, it was not until he was walking to his car the next morning, after receiving assurances from the doctor his dad would make it, that he even thought of the old man. He went to the trailer park and the convenience store searching for the old Indian. He stopped by the store on his way to the hospital each morning and again on his way back to the RV each evening. No one seemed willing to tell him where the old man lived. They wouldn't even give him his name. He realized too late and with a guilty conscience that he had not asked it of the old Indian.

With the help of a mechanic, he got the RV running again. He moved it to Red Rock State Park and rented a space for the next week. The nice couple who operated the Trading Post were invaluable in their assistance in getting the RV ready. They helped him clean out all the filth. The three of them would sit up late into the night talking. They would only nod their heads and smile whenever he brought up the old Indian and his whereabouts. The day came when they were ready to leave. After saying goodbye to them, he pulled slowly out onto the main road leading to I-40.

Heading east, he enjoyed the view of the red rocks. He saw a lone figure standing on top of a solitary hill. The figure was too far away to make out, yet he knew. A slow wave from the old Indian brought a heavy lump to his throat. "Thank you," he whispered under his breath.

After four days of easy driving, they pulled into his parents' house late in the evening. They did not bother to unload anything. Both men were too tired to lift anything until the next day. The trip had taken almost a week. His dad's health had improved during this time. His dad had even helped with the driving for the past two days. He seemed more like his old self now, talking and at times even joking a little.

After spending several more days with his dad, he knew with reluctance it was time for him to go. His supervisor had been more than generous giving him the time off, and almost three weeks had passed. There was nothing more he could do. The neighbors would look in on pops. His dad's spirit seemed to be getting better each day. He would call him daily to check on him. His dad promised to visit him in a couple of weeks. A long goodbye hug, and he was on his way back to D.C. His last look in the rearview mirror showed his dad standing in the driveway, waving slowly. His shoulders stooped from some inner weight he was forced to carry. "I know, dad," he said to himself. "We both miss her."

He had nightmares. He woke at times, and the bedding was drenched in sweat. He would get up, make a pot of coffee, and then watch the news on TV until the sun came up. He didn't pay attention to the commentator. He was lost in his thoughts about her last words to him in the desert. What did she mean? What did she mean, "Our son needs your help"? Was something going to happen to his boy? He tried to push the thought from his mind, yet it kept returning time and time again.

They talked on the phone almost every night. There were several nights when his son was working and couldn't call. On these nights, the old neighbors down the street always managed to stop by and spend time with him. He knew his son had made preplanned arrangements with them to do so.

He started running again. He was up to three miles and feeling better each day. And he would eat the food his neighbors brought over. Often they did cookouts on the grill. His good friends and neighbors came over almost weekly. They would play cards or checkers or dominoes. His weight was up, and his complexion looked better. The nightly phone calls from his son were a big boost. They had made plans to spend a long weekend together. He would drive up to D.C., and the two of them would take in several movies and go to a comedy club.

Several months passed; his medication for extreme depression began to have a positive effect. But the weekend visits with his son had better results than any prescription. Gradually, he began to heal. There was still a spark of life that he could enjoy—not to the extent he had with his wife but he still had his son. He was the one thing that gave his life a glimmer of hope. Someday, too, there might be a daughter-in-law and a grandson or granddaughter. That day might even come sooner than he expected. During one of their phone calls his son had told him about a girl he had met.

"I think she might be the one, dad. I want you to meet her when you come up next week. She is really looking forward to meeting you."

They had spent a nice weekend together. He was mildly surprised, meeting the girl of his son's dreams. She had long dark hair and looked a lot like his son's grandmother. Her eyes were large and open. Her sense of humor was light and funny. But her eyes—those big, brown, loving eyes reminded him so much of his mother's.

Within minutes of the introductions, the two of them were laughing and sharing stories about his boy. He relaxed and heaved a happy sigh. This young lady was the perfect woman for his son. They plotted with great secrecy a few jokes they would pull on his son the next time they got together. Her hug goodbye was full of warmth and caring. He liked her. He felt a bond develop between the two of them, and he knew they would become closer in time. The two of them stood in the driveway, waving goodbye, arms around each other in a natural embrace. The short weekend ended all too soon. He drove away with a happy heart.

At his son's insistence, he went in for a check-up.

"Nothing to worry about, just a cold that's been hanging on." It was the infrequent coughing spells doing their conversations that had alerted his son. He had spent the day in a doctor's office, being poked and prodded. He was given a series of blood tests and x-rays. The doctor told him he would call in a few days if there was anything to worry about. He would call his son tonight to let him know that he had the check-up. Now the boy would quit hounding him about it. He was whistling an old military tune when he walked into the house. The phone was ringing as he entered the door.

"Hello!" he said in a cheerful voice.

"Sir, I have some bad news for you. This is your son's immediate supervisor from the FBI. I'm sorry to have to inform you that your son has been shot. Can you please come as soon as possible?"

He entered the emergency room with lead feet and with an aching heart. He saw everything in one crystal clear pattern. The nurses' white uniforms and the fluorescent lights were so bright they seemed violent against his eyes. His head was pounding. He had to concentrate to understand what was being said to him. His son was still alive, but it was very critical. He had been sprayed with a nine- millimeter machine gun. They had removed the bullets that penetrated his body. Two were left in his left lung. One round broke the bone in his left forearm. They had just finished removing several bullets in his lower leg and began placing pins in the compound fracture in his shinbone. The doctor did not know if he would live. They were fighting off the infection now and trying to keep the fluid from building up in his lungs. If he could make it through the night he might have a chance.

"Could I see him?" His jaw quivered.

The boy's supervisor, who had called him, came up and shook his hand. "There are no words to even express how sorry I am, sir. I know this must be very difficult for you, especially now that your wife is gone. . . ."

"How did this happen?" He wanted to scream. He wanted to tear at the walls with his bare hands. But he remained calm

"Your son was a part of a team doing surveillance on a car theft ring," the supervisor told him. "They had been stealing late model Caprice Classics and shipping them to Saudi Arabia. Since many of the stolen cars had crossed various state lines, we were called in. They had located a warehouse being used to store the vehicles, and the local police had raided the place. Your son was there to observe. He was standing out of the way, allowing the local police and SWAT teams to make the arrest. One of the Saudis made a run for it. He jumped into a car and crashed through a set of double doors. He wasn't a very good driver. He crashed into another building and killed his engine. Your son thought, as we all did, this was the end of the situation. The streets were blocked off, and there was no way for the guy to escape. He walked up to within fifteen feet of the Saudi who was still trying to start his car. We heard your son say, 'Step out of the car. You are surrounded,' when the idiot pulled out a gun and started shooting. It happened so fast no one could react in time. The Saudi was taken into custody, but I'm afraid he will be on the next plane home in just a few hours. He was checked out. He . . . he . . . has diplomatic immunity. I'm sorry sir. We did not perceive anything like this happening."

He was escorted into his son's room. He tried to understand how his son could be lying there, shot to pieces and dying over a used car. His son was sleeping. The wires and tubes attached to his body sent a shock through him. He slowly walked up to his son and gently took his hand. He leaned over the bed, being careful not to touch his little boy. He whispered, "I'm here, son." There was no response. He stood that way through the long night. He watched the heart monitor's steady beat. He prayed that his heart would stay strong. He moved only when a nurse came in periodically to change an IV bag.

The sun was about to crown the horizon when a loud screeching noise blared from one of the machines. He could see the lines on the monitor jump in an uneven pattern. A nurse was there within seconds, followed closely by a doctor. He stood there dazed until he was roughly shoved away by the doctor who was barking orders inbetween a stream of curses. He slowly backed out of the room. He continued staring at the doctor pounding on his son's chest. The lines on the monitor returned to one final unwavering line.

He knew that he had lost the last thing in this world that meant anything to him. He braced himself against a wall. It took all his remaining strength just to hold himself upright.

"Forgive me, son. I failed you." He stumbled down the corridor, wiping the tears from his eyes. His head was down. He didn't see the young woman with dark hair, curled up asleep in a waiting room chair.

He stood outside the hospital taking deep breaths, trying to clear his head. He took in as much air as his lungs could stand. But he couldn't hold it in. He shook violently with helplessness. He held his head with both hands and hoped to get some order in his mind. But there were only screams and a high-pitched banging. The pounding in his head grew louder and louder. Image followed image through his grieving mind. His life flashed through his addled memory. The beatings he withstood in school, the kids laughing at him for wearing old clothes, for wearing his hair long. "Run! Run!" They yelled in mock terror. "There's a mad Indian loose. Run! Or he will scalp you. Don't trade with him! He's an Indian giver! Indian giver! Indian giver!" They would chant over and over. "Indian's always steal! Don't leave anything he can get to or he will steal it."

His desk was always the first one to be searched if something came up missing in the classroom. The teachers treated him as less than a human. They used him as a source of amusement for the class. They laughed at his beliefs, at what he knew to be true because his mother told him. They laughed because his people had come out of the ground. His entire life was spent living around people with no respect for him. He was forced into believing that he was dumb. He was forced to bend under their will. Years of thinking he was just a dumb Indian. Not good enough to even speak to a white girl. The beatings he suffered if a white girl would smile at him.

He did not belong in this white man's world. They had showed him time and time again that he was not good enough. His mother died at the hands of two pieces of white trash. The memory of his childhood surged back. Memories he had suppressed his whole life filtered through his mind. He watched his father breaking his back to make a living, struggling because of his love for an Indian.

His mind stopped. The blue-checkered shirt! His father's arm had been wrapped in a dirty blue-checkered shirt not long after his mother died! His father did not sit back and allow a weak court system to punish those responsible. That dirty blue-checkered cloth had come from the man who had killed his mother.

What did he have to show for a life of misery, pain, and insults? He fought and scraped all his life to make a living so that he could have a family. But it was all taken away. He tried to prove that he was an equal. He had abused his body and endured unimaginable conditions to serve his country. What did he have to show for his struggles? His years of serving his country were supposed to allow him to live and prosper. Why did he ever think he could have the great American dream?

His wife had been taken from him. The justice system had done nothing to her killer. There was no happiness in this world. He had spent years trying to fit in, years trying to prove he was as good as they were. His life and the ones he loved meant nothing to those in power. They could take whatever they wanted from him at any time, and they paid nothing. Nothing for taking his wife. Nothing for taking his mother. And now his son. His last chance, his last hope for a family. They all would pay. He was born an Indian, now it was time to fight back like one. As his ancestors would have done. He knew he would lose, but he still had to fight them. He would make them all suffer for what the system had done to him, to his family.

A shudder went through his entire body. A cold sweat came over him. His mind finally snapped. More and more memories flooded his conscious. They called me an Indian giver in school, it's time I become what they believe me to be. I will show them what this Indian can give them. He started walking. He formulated his plan as he moved along the busy sidewalk. He was unaware of the life going on around him.

"Where did he go?" The doctor asked the nurse at the night desk.

"I think he went outside." The doctor walked to the door and looked up and down the street. He didn't see the boy's father, so he walked back to the nurse's desk.

"Tell him when he comes back, his son is ok. Still in for a bumpy ride, but I think he will make it. His fever has just broken, and he's resting now."

The young woman, who had been asleep in the waiting room chair, heard the doctor's conversation with the nurse.

"Thank you, Lord," she cried.

Instead of flying back home, he rented a car. He needed time to think, to use what this country had taught him. He would inflict as much pain as they had given him. He would even the score by using what they had taught him.

The plan slowly began to congeal. The thought crossed his mind as he drove through the mid-morning hours. By the time he pulled into the driveway of his home, most of the details were in place. He didn't bother going into the house. There were too many memories lingering in the walls. His savings account was still packed away in the RV. He still had all of his wife's life insurance policy. The only time he had used any of it was to buy a new suit. He retrieved the savings account book and placed it in the rental car. He went to the garage and came back with a five-gallon can of gasoline. He placed it on the rear steps and picked up a rake he had left by the door. He broke every window on the back side of the house before pouring the contents of the can into the back bedroom. He grabbed an emergency flare and struck it. He tossed it into the window. As he walked away, he heard a muffled whumpff.

He was once again burning the past. He turned onto the highway heading west. His destination and plans were finalized. He was twenty miles down the road, so he didn't hear the sirens wailing behind him.

The one military post he knew and disliked the most was Fort Leonard Wood, Missouri. Fort Leonard Wood was established as an engineer training post at the onset of World War II, and it had remained the same for the past sixty years. Soldiers were known to have taken basic training there and retire after twenty years, never leaving for an overseas assignment. The disadvantage of this was the amount of non-commissioned officers that thought they were superior sergeants because they wore spit-shined boots and heavily-starched fatigues. After years of trainees and privates jumping at their every command, some of them actually believed they were the Army's best leaders. Their egos inflated, they were out of touch with the real Army. He could identify their type at a glance. They would give a poor private all kinds of grief, yet bend over backwards to kiss a superior's ass. These were the very ones he would seek out for assistance. They would, he believed, break a few minor rules if there were any possibility of advancing their careers. In doing so, they would seal the fate of the United States.

Driving onto the open post, he was waved through by two military police soldiers, too busy talking to each other to notice that he did not have a post sticker. It wouldn't have mattered if they had stopped him. All he needed to do was to show them his retired military identification card and he would have been waved through. He had gotten a haircut at one of the local barbershops just off post. His freshly cut hair gave him the appearance of a soldier once again.

His first stop was at the military clothing and sales store, a place where anyone with an active military I.D. could purchase new uniforms. He entered the main entrance and selected an officer's set of dress greens and a pair of shoes. After filling a small hand basket with the rank of a full colonel and various awards and decorations, he went to the check-out line. Everyone was required to show an I.D. at the checkout. The cashier's job was to check each I.D. to ensure a soldier did not do the very thing that he was doing, buying something he was not authorized to wear. If he had been challenged, he prepared a cover story: He was purchasing the items of clothing for an old retired friend who was going to receive a long overdue award. Since his friend, the colonel, was retired and in a wheel chair, did she want him to go get him? But he was not challenged. The cashier had worked a long day and was anxious to get home. He made sure he was the last customer and that most the entrance doors had already been locked. The look on her face was one of boredom. She just wanted him to leave as soon as possible. He paid in cash and left the building, walking casually to the door. His next stop was an alteration place off post. He had the uniform measured and cut to fit him. He put in a rush order. He had to pay more, but he could pick it up the next day. He drove to a nearby motel and, after getting a room, went to bed. Phase one of his plan had been completed.

The next day he wore a colonel's uniform, waiting comfortably in an easy chair while his new military I.D. card was being processed. The staff sergeant was more than willing to make him an I.D. card after hearing the story of how someone had stolen his wallet.

"Could you hurry, sergeant?" He asked in an impatient voice. "I've still got to cancel my credit cards."

"Yes, sir!" The young staff sergeant knew anyone needing an I.D. card was supposed to have the proper paperwork from his unit. But this guy was a colonel! Just one rank below a general! The young soldier was not about to jeopardize his short career by upsetting what was obviously an already upset officer. "Here you are, sir!" The staff sergeant said. He handed him a card with his recently taken picture. "I'm sorry you had to wait so long. I hope you find your wallet." Not bothering to thank him, he took the card and left. The young staff sergeant's voice trailed after him. "If your wallet was stolen, I hope they catch the guy who took it! Have a nice day, sir."

He stood off to the side, observing the master sergeant in charge of passports give a young soldier and his wife an unusually difficult time. The higher-ranking sergeant seemed to take particular delight in treating the young soldier with complete disrespect. He was deliberately humiliating the young man in front of his wife. He told him to return to his unit and have someone with half a brain help him fill out the paperwork. The master sergeant gave the young soldier's wife a leering stare as they departed, making it obvious to her what was on his mind.

After the young couple left with a look of helplessness, the master sergeant turned to the full bird colonel standing off to the side. The officer must have had a cold coming on. He had a persistent cough, not loud, just a little annoying. "How may I help you, sir?" The master sergeant said with a huge smile. His voice was saturated with respect.

He told him, "I've been observing you soldier. I like the way you treated that dumb private. You're just the kind of man I've been looking for."

"Yes, sir! Thank you, sir!" Fifteen minutes later, he left the in-processing center with a new passport. He drove off the post and onto the interstate. He was headed east. His mission at Fort Leonard Wood was complete. His next stop was New York City. From there, he could catch a flight to Germany. Now that he was back in the Army, he would fly at government expense. The government would not only pay for his airfare, they would also provide him with a small suitcase, a briefcase that had more explosive power than the two bombs dropped on Japan combined. He lit a cigarette and, after several puffs, had to toss it out the window, the smoke irritated his lungs. They seemed to have grown more sensitive in the past few days.

CHAPTER 25

She was there when he opened his eyes, sitting in a chair beside his bed.

"What am I doing here?" His mind was still groggy from the anesthetic. His voice was hoarse from the tubes down his throat.

"Hi, baby," she replied. She didn't trust her voice to say anything else. She held his hand, caressing it as she had done continuously for the past four days. He tried to turn but felt a stabbing pain shoot through his chest. There was an oxygen tube blowing cool air up his nose. It was helping him breathe. It irritated his nose, making it sensitive and dry. He opened his eyes again and saw her sitting there beside him.

"How long have I been here?" he asked.

"About four days. You've been coming in and out of it for the last couple days. Your fever broke last night. The doctor said you were one hell of a fighter. Of course, I could have told him that. Now you just lay there and get better. I need you. I'm in love with you, so you better listen to me. I'll open a can of whoop ass and pour it on you if you don't."

He smiled at the threat, the very same one his dad had used in front of her. His dad even gave her a class. He showed her how to open it and pour it over his head if he ever did anything that displeased her in the slightest way. He smiled at the memory of the two of them picking on him.

"Where's pop?" She hesitated for a split second before giving him an answer. She had never lied to him before and didn't want to start now. But she knew she had to or he wouldn't get well.

"He's been standing here beside you for the last four days. He just left to get a shower and a few hours sleep. He told me to tell you he will see you in the morning. He wanted me to tell you that he loves you very much. Now, enough talking. You close those green eyes and get some sleep. I'll be here when you wake up."

He nodded his head and fell back into a painful sleep. She stayed for another hour before quietly leaving the room. For the first time since her arrival at the hospital, she allowed tears of joy to overtake her emotionally drained body. He was going to live! She went to the chapel on the bottom floor and thanked God. Exhausted, she eventually made it to her car. The short drive to her apartment took longer than usual. She drove cautiously. She was afraid of falling asleep and getting into an accident. But she needed to get home.

Once inside her apartment, she made a phone call to her future father-in-law's house. The phone rang until the answering machine picked up. She left a message. "Your son is doing fine. I hope everything is ok with you. Please call me and let us know where you are. I can't delay telling him that you're missing, I don't want to lie to your son. I'll have to tell him something. Well, there's not too much else to say. . . . I love you, old man." She hung up reluctantly.

After taking her first shower in four days, she thought she would fall asleep instantly. But for some reason, she couldn't sleep. She was filled with so much emotion. The unknown kept floating through her tired mind. It took all the strength she had not to think about what she might have lost.

He awoke as the night nurse took his pulse and gave him his pill. He had to drink several times to get it down his throat.

"What did I just take?"

"Just a sleeping pill to help you relax," she replied. He groaned inwardly. The pain began to climb now that he was fully awake. He wanted to ask the nurse, "Why the hell didn't you just let me sleep? Why did you wake me up to give me a damn sleeping pill, you moron?"

Instead, he said, "Thank you," adjusting himself as far as his constraints would allow him. He slowly fell into a fitful sleep.

He began to dream. At first he had the same recurring nightmare of an Arab slowly raising a gun and firing point blank at him. The impact of the bullets flung him backwards like a rag doll. The Arab got out of his car and walked toward him in a slow, deliberate motion as he slowly lifted his submachine gun. The Arab's eyes resembled two black shiny pits. It reminded him of his fear of snakes. As long as he could remember, he had been deathly afraid of snakes. The Arab's head became a rattlesnake, its mouth opening to expose fangs dripping with poison. It reared back to strike him. He couldn't move. None of his muscles would respond. The head leaped towards him. Then it became a blur, but it sped closer to him. It turned its head sideways to sink its deadly teeth into his exposed flesh. His body tensed, awaiting the impact. His eyes froze. They were unable to close. He watched, wide eyed, as the menacing teeth sank deep into his chest. The snake recoiled for another bite and struck him again. As the snake coiled for a third time, his father was there. He cut the snake's head off in mid-air when it flew at lightning speed towards him.

He was sixteen again. His father had taken him on a week-long camping trip. The two of them had returned to his father's place of birth and spent the day searching for his grandparents' graves. They found the burial site after several hours of looking. The underbrush and saplings had covered them completely. They spent the afternoon clearing the graves and carving new markers for his grandmother, grandfather, and his aunt. That night over a small campfire his dad told him how his sister had died. He missed her, even though he never had known her. He missed her because of the stories his father had told him about her. His dad told him of his childhood and how difficult it was. He told him how strange life had seemed growing up in this remoteness. This land now belonged to them, left to him by his father, as it had been left to his father and his father before him. The land had been in the family for several hundred years. Soon it would belong to him.

"You must never sell this land," his father said, sweeping his arms in a wide arc to signify the acres. It was too rocky and isolated to grow anything or be worth much. Yet it bordered the Indian reservation where his grandmother was born. "Keep this land for our future generations. Perhaps at some point in time they may need to live here. There are many wild animals, and a man could survive here if he needed to." He fell silent. Confidently he spoke again, "This is a sanctuary. A place that is safe from outside harm." He didn't know what his father meant by that.

The next day they had begun a four-day fast. They drank only water and built a sweat lodge. They collected the rocks that would provide the steam. After purifying themselves in a nearby stream, they built a fire and placed the rocks in it to be heated. His father taught him how to enter the sweat lodge and where to sit. The rocks were brought in, carried on two antlers, and placed into the hole that he had dug into the ground in the middle of the room. The door flap was closed, and slowly his father began pouring water over the heated rocks. A cloud of steam rose with the mixture of wood ashes. It filled his nostrils with a smell that was foreign, yet somehow familiar.

They spent several hours inside the sweat lodge. He sat in the total darkness listening to his father pray softly. His father would wet the rocks, and the hot steam would pour forth. His body was covered with a fine mixture of ashes and moisture. As he sat listening to his father speak to the Great Spirit, he could not fathom what was taking place inside the sweat lodge. The lodge seemed to fill with other beings. His father maintained his quiet chant. Each time his dad placed new hot rocks into the hole and poured water over them, he seemed to drift closer and closer to these spirits. Looking deep into the pit of rocks, he saw one of them split in half. Inside, he saw a face begin to appear. It was the face of his grandmother. He stared at his grandmother. He felt a bond weld between them. She was telling him, somehow, how much she loved him and how proud she was of her grandson. Although he did not hear these words, he knew that she had spoken them. His grandmother's image stayed inside the rock until her face faded along with the heat. The experience for him was something he knew he would never forget. He felt pride as they came out of the lodge. He felt the presence of his Indian ancestors near him. His body felt warm from the moist heat of the sweat lodge. He was extremely proud of his father and proud to have Indian blood running through his veins.

They fasted for four days, drinking only water. On the fourth day, he no longer felt hunger pains, just as his father had told him. They entered the sweat lodge again, and he felt a sense of urgency to see his grandmother again—if she should appear. For now, there wasn't a thing to do but relax and wait for darkness.

He took a walk around the land where his father grew up. He stumbled on a small stream with a large oak tree. The tree was strong. It had large roots dipping into the bank. There was a pleasant area under the tree, a soft, plush mound of grass that seemed to beckon him to lie down. He stretched out, a sigh escaping his lips. The ground made contact with his back. The place felt so natural to him. He was daydreaming. He watched the clouds change shapes and sizes. They flirted with each other over a clear blue sky. Only God could make something so magnificent. He drifted off to sleep under the warm sun. He dreamed of his grandmother. He saw her smile at him. She told him what a handsome young man he was. She smiled and said how much he looked like her son. She told him she was sorry for not living long enough to be with him, but that she was happy on the other side. His grandfather stepped up next to her. He placed his arm around her. He smiled. He wondered why his grandfather's face was one of sadness. He didn't have time to ask him before his grandfather spoke. The words he spoke weren't clear. The image of the two of them began to fade away into a misty shroud of fog. The only words he understood came almost as a shout, "Remember the field! The field!"

He told his dad about his dream. When he told him what his grandfather had said, his father looked puzzled. There was a field not too far from here. They decided to go look at it, to see if there was something there that they should know about. It was easy to find. They walked in an easterly direction and came out almost dead center in a large field. It was a flat piece of ground surrounded by trees. The grass had been recently mowed.

"Someone has been using this as a runway," his father remarked. "I wonder what they are doing here." They walked up and down the grassy slope. From what his dad could remember, this was on the very edge of their property. His dad made a rough estimate and decided that the trees on the eastern side of the runway were the boundary line. It was not on his land, so it was none of their business. They returned to camp. He could not shake the anxiety he felt from his grandfather's warning. I wonder what he was trying to tell me.

That night his father told him stories about his grandfather and grandmother. His dad's low voice and the sound of the forest brought a feeling of closeness between them. He realized that the past several days had tightened an already strong bond between them, a bond that could never be severed by this world. He looked at his father across the dim fire light, and he saw a friend that would be there for him anytime or anywhere. He made a silent vow to be the same kind of friend to his dad.

A gentle hand touched his. He opened his eyes; she was there sitting beside him. Her eyes were red from an obvious lack of sleep. There was a small mascara smear under the corner of her right eye, and her hair was still damp from her recent shower. She is so beautiful, he smiled.

"Hi gorgeous!" Her tired face lit up.

"How is my man feeling today?" The excitement in her voice sprung out with each word. She leaned over carefully, avoiding all his bumps and bruises. She kissed him softly. He felt her hesitation. His immediate supervisor walked through the door.

"What have we here?" He demanded. "I came in feeling sorry for your ugly butt, and what do I find? You laying there, taking a kiss from a young lady. I bet there's not a thing wrong with you. This is just your way of taking a vacation at the government expense."

Turning to her, he said in a solemn tone that made her giggle. "I hope this peace of camel dung has not been trying to take advantage of you. He's a sly devil who cannot be trusted under any circumstances!"

Then looking at him, he said, relieved, "It's good to see those eyes open. You sure had a lot of people worried."

He made an attempt to raise his hand but thought better of it and said, "Hi, boss. It's good to see you too." They talked small talk for a while. His supervisor checked his watch and excused himself for some pressing business. He could know that the two of them needed to be alone. The supervisor's querying look at her and the small shake of her head confirmed the missing link had not shown up. I'll tell him, her eyes responded. Saying his goodbyes, he promised to return later. He left the two lovers holding hands.

"Your supervisor has been worried about you," she said after he left the room. "He's been here night and day driving the nurses crazy."

"I'm a lucky man."

She knew it was coming. "Has my dad been here?"

She could no longer lie to him. She cried, "Your father left the hospital when you were brought in. He left thinking the worst, that you were dead. I haven't heard from him or seen him. I can't get hold of him. I didn't want to say anything sooner because I've just been hoping that he'd show up. I'm sorry. I don't know what else to say."

His dad was out there somewhere thinking he was dead. What could be going through his poor, tortured mind? He remembered his dad's condition when he had found him in the desert, the pain and turmoil he had gone through after his mother's brutal death. Deep in his heart he knew his father was living because of him. He had to get hold of him as soon as possible. There was no telling what he might do.

"Do me a favor, honey Go to my apartment, and in my phone directory you'll find dad's neighbors. Call them and see what you can find out." She promised him she would.

A nurse came in with a fresh bottle of IV solution and another sleeping pill. The nurse asked her to leave for a while and let him get some rest. She gave him a long kiss and caressed his damp forehead, then she left. She promised to return in the evening.

He watched her leave thinking he was, indeed, a very lucky man. The sleeping pill began to take its effect. His body relaxed, and he fell asleep.

The numerous camping trips the three of them took whenever there was time, his dad teaching about the animals in the woods, and the need for respecting life had stayed with him throughout his life. His dad taught him to kill animals for food, to never take a life needlessly, nor waste anything that he killed. They rarely did any hunting with a gun. His dad showed him how to make traps and snares for small animals. He also taught him how to make a bow and arrows for the larger ones.

He was seventeen. They had been stationed back at Fort Bragg for almost a year. His birthday present was a total surprise. He and his dad were going to take flying lessons together. They both ganged up on mom, begging her to join them. She would have none of it. No, she was happy to stay on the ground. She'd spent enough time in the air, going back and forth overseas, to last her a lifetime.

The flying lessons became an obsession for the two of them. They spent hours pouring over magazines and books about flying. They both flew solo on the same day. Mom had packed a nice lunch, which they all enjoyed at the end of the small grass runway. The summer sun was bright, and the rolling mountains of white clouds made dancing shadows around them. Mom was not crazy about the two of them flying. She was happy that her two men were enjoying something together. She never tired of seeing the excitement in their eyes. Green dancing devils or green-eyed monsters, she fondly called them. He and his dad had made friends with most of the pilots. Just when mom thought their flying lessons were done, the two of them burst through the door with the news they would soon be qualified on a Baron multi-engine. An old pilot at the airfield offered to train them for the price of fuel and some carpentry work on his house.

A week after getting their multi-engine license, the two of them took mom for a ride. They had finally broken her will. She seemed nervous on the take-off but said nothing as he banked the plane on her side and climbed to 8000 feet.

"Don't you love it, mom?" he asked her excitedly. "This plane can go higher than thirty thousand feet."

"Don't you dare!" she screeched, panicked.

"I suppose there are worse things you two could be doing," she had said with a shudder. "You could have taken up sky-diving." It was all she could do to watch her husband fall through the air. She didn't think she could stand both of them doing something so dangerous.

They pestered her relentlessly day and night, pleading and begging to allow them to buy an airplane.

"No. Our money is being saved for a house. We can't live in a plane, and I'm tired of living on a military post. Not to mention your college tuition. We will just barely make the payments at that school you want to attend. Now don't bother me anymore about a plane. You two will just have to rent a plane when you have the money." No amount of persuasion would change her mind.

He was seventeen when they finally moved into their own house. He and his dad had located it on the days they left mom home. The two of them felt so guilty about their selfish behavior and their constant nagging that they both agreed to give up flying and find mom a house. They knew they had found the right house when the realtor had showed them this one. It was several miles outside of the city limits. Large pine trees lined a long driveway that circled in front of a three-car garage. There were neighbors close by, but not too close.

The three acres of land would keep mom busy for years, planting flowers and landscaping. He and dad did not know it at the time, but they would provide the sweaty labor with picks, shovels, and wheelbarrels full of rocks and dirt. In the following years they'd tease her, pretending to be sick or injured whenever she started a new project. Sometimes the two of them would hide like little kids, and she would wander around the house and yard calling for them to come out. "No work, no eat," she would say. They would come out of hiding once she was out of sight. Good hiding places were getting hard to come by. His mom had gotten better over the years at finding them. When she did, she always went for the ears, pulling her two men over to the next construction site. Then she would stand there like a drill sergeant barking orders.

The day came when the two of them would surprise her. They woke mom up early and served her breakfast in bed. She knew something was up but decided to play along. After breakfast, she was escorted to the bathroom where a tub of hot water had been poured with her favorite bubbles. Her blue jeans and blouse were hung on the rack with instructions for her to get dressed after she enjoyed her bath. She noticed they had forgotten to include underwear and a bra.

"Where are we going?"

"Today is your day, mom, so just sit back and relax." His dad drove the car and turned up the radio whenever she tried to pry any information from him. After twisting his ear, she got dad to turn the radio down. He sat in the back seat laughing at his dad's fake howls of pain. She could not help but have a good time. Soon the three of them were laughing. They pulled onto a side road from the main highway, a road she had traveled on several times. She had driven down this road once with a realtor who showed her the perfect house. It had a long driveway with tall pine trees leading all the way up to the house. She drove by many times to look at it and daydream about how she would fix up. She told the realtor it was what she wanted, but they couldn't afford it. They looked at other houses, but none could measure up to that one.

They were coming up on the house now. Her heart sank when she saw a sold emblem covering the for sale sign. Hope whoever bought it treats it as good as I would have. As his dad pulled into the driveway he was watching his mom's face in the rearview mirror.

At first she tried to protest, saying it was too expensive. There was no way they could afford this house and send him to college. That's when his dad spoke up in his quiet voice and told her that the boy had decided to attend a local college. So the money they had been saving for him to go away to college had made the down payment. She started to protest all the more on hearing this. It was his turn to interject and rescue his dad.

"Mom, it was my idea. Don't blame dad," he said. "I want you to have this place. Besides, I can't pass up living here either. But since it's so far out in the country, you're gonna have to extend my curfew." The look she gave him told him he said the right thing. She grabbed him and covered his face with kisses. Then she hugged his dad.

"How did you know about this place?" She asked him.

"The realtor." The three of them walked up the driveway together arm in arm. He had never seen his mom so happy. Her face was blushing from joy. Her eyes were so alive. For the first time since he was a baby, she actually walking faster than he. A sidelong glance from his dad, and the two of them slowed their walk to a crawl. "If you two ever want to eat another meal you better stop it!"

She was there in the evening when he opened his eyes. She looked worried. He instinctively knew it must be about his father.

"Did you call the neighbors?"

"Yes," she replied. "Someone tried to burn your house down, but your neighbors managed to put the fire out before the fire department arrived. The damage was contained to the back two bedrooms. Your neighbors were having a walk after dinner and saw a strange car parked in your driveway. They couldn't see who was driving it. They saw the flames, and put it out with a water hose. You've got some really nice neighbors. They boarded the house up and have been keeping an eye on the place." She paused a little too long.

"What else?"

"Well . . . whoever started the fire also had keys to the shed where the gasoline was stored. The RV is still in the driveway, and your dad's car was found in the airport parking lot. It's been sitting there since he had flew up to D.C. to see you in the hospital."

The two of them held hands. There was nothing more she could tell him, nothing more she could think of to ease his worry. She sat quietly sharing in his sorrow. She wished she could wipe his troubles away. But she knew all she could do was to sit quietly and let him know she was there for him.

The nurse came in and gave her a ten-minute warning. "You can see him tomorrow, honey. We're kicking him out of intensive care. We need the bed for people who are actually sick!" The two of them laughed.

She gave him a kiss and whispered, "I love you." She headed for the door. Glancing over her shoulder, she saw the look of concern return to his boyish face. "See you tomorrow!"

She left feeling helpless and a little guilty to be the bearer of bad news. As she drove home she was angry with his dad. She was still concerned, but why hadn't he contacted anyone? Was he out there somewhere all alone? What must he be thinking? She felt a small tinge of regret for her feelings.

The C-130 aircraft came to a bumpy landing at the Frankfort Airport. It taxied slowly to the U.S. terminal, and after the engines were shut down the passengers were permitted to unload. The slight drizzle of cold rain falling on the Tar-Mac gave a dreary welcome to the passengers as they shuffled through the unprotected elements to the terminal. Once inside, the passengers passed through customs. The German guards had no reason to inspect the military passengers from a military plane. Even if they had, they wouldn't have questioned the colonel about the forty-five automatic in his suitcase.

He paused long enough in the terminal to exchange his American dollars for German marks to buy a sandwich. Within an hour of landing, he was on a train heading toward his final destination. He was on his way to his old duty station. He was going to a much happier time in his life, a place in the past with a loving wife and a wonderful son, a place in the past where he had once been the highest ranking non-commissioned officer in charge of the Special Forces nuclear arsenal.

He changed into civilian clothes and took special care to pack his uniform so it wouldn't wrinkle. He wouldn't need it for another four days.

As he watched the small towns and hamlets pass by from the window of the train, his mind started to wander to that other time. The walks they took in the early morning through the mountains around Bad Tolz. He remembered the ski trips the three of them cherished and looked forward to throughout the year. He recalled the warm nights holding her in his arms and watching her breath softly on his chest. He shook his head. There was no time to dwell on something that could never be again. There was no past! He had to concentrate on the future. He had to plan the final phase of his operation.

This would be the most difficult part, getting his hands on the suit-case locked in a basement four stories underground. It was surrounded by cameras and hypersensitive sound devices. The suitcase he was going to steal was secured behind doors two feet thick. A code word was necessary to get close to the massive doors that in turn required two keys to open. The keys must also be turned at the exact same time from fifteen feet away in order for the doors to open. There were many obstacles he had to overcome. A voice-monitored safe contained both keys, and the password to open the safe was known only to the battalion commander and the battalion executive officer. All steps covering this security had been tested time and again. He knew them by heart, because he was once in charge of testing them. It would be impossible to get the passwords from the battalion commander or his assistant. He knew these men would die rather than give up a nuclear bomb, regardless of the torture or threats. He had spent enough time in Special Forces to know getting the password from any soldier was not plausible. No, he would have to attack this problem from another angle. It would require a great deal of luck on his part and a small amount of neglect in security on the Army's.

He spent his time dozing and going over his final plan during the six-hour train ride. He carried with him his last pack of cigarettes. He couldn't help reliving the past when he looked at those cigarettes. He had made a promise to her years ago that he would quit before he died. He had said it in a joking mood, one that he had quickly regretted when he saw the look of despair cross her lovely face.

"All right, honey," he told her as he placed his arms around her waist. "I will quit on our trip around the United States. But you have to promise to help keep my mind occupied with other things."

She turned around slowly and kissed him before whispering, "Do you want a cigarette right this minute?"

"What is a cigarette?" He whispered back. He picked her up and carried her into the bedroom. He did not smoke a cigarette again until late the next morning.

He was forced to shake his head furiously to rid himself of the unbearable image of his past. He stood up somewhat shakily from his seat. He walked to the dining car and ordered a cup of coffee. He lit up a smoke and took several puffs before he put it out. His chest hurt when he breathed. The smoke from the cigarette seemed to make it worse.

Finishing his coffee, he went back to his semi-private quarters. He forced himself to lie down. After several hours, he fell into a restless sleep. His nagging cough woke him several times during the night. But before the morning, he fell into a deep, exhausted sleep. The sun peeked through the several small windows in the train car. A small dribble of saliva slipped from the corner of his mouth and slid down his cheek. It left a dark red stain on the pillow.

He was finally being released from the hospital. He was in considerable pain and extremely weak, but the doctor said he had a fast recovery. She wheeled him slowly through the hospital corridor. The automatic door opened, and a cold gust of freezing rain slapped him in the face. She readjusted the blanket around him and pushed the wheelchair to her car. She fumbled briefly with the chair brake before opening the passenger door. Another gust of cold wind attacked them, and her dress flew up around her ears. The wind was flirting with her long black hair. It tossed and twisted it across her rosy cheeks and nose. Damn, she's pretty.

She quickly held his good arm. He struggled to get in her small car. The leg cast posed their biggest challenge. He was finally seated and only in a small amount of pain. He watched in amazement as she closed his door. She ran the wheelchair back inside and threw herself in the car. Before she put the key in the ignition, she turned towards him with a smile. He couldn't help but laugh.

"What's so funny?"

"Just enjoy watching you flutter about. Reminds me of a mother bird looking after one of her chicks." She chuckled.

She started the car and tuned the heater on high. It wasn't long before she began to chatter about everything and nothing in her happy way. He sat listening to her, enjoying the various tones of her voice. He loved watching her uncontrolled expressions that followed each comment. He wondered how she managed to drive using her hands to emphasize each word.

She had moved some of her things into his apartment. She would stay with him until he got better. She knew that he had no one to look after him. To her relief, he didn't object. She had never met anyone who was so self-reliant. He was willing to help a perfect stranger anytime, but for some reason he didn't want to ask for help himself. She recognized this early on in their relationship. He would do anything for her, but he was uncomfortable if she wanted to return the favor. After meeting his father, she realized where he got it from.

Life was a never-ending adventure for her. She saw beauty in everything. He sat back in the seat and listened to her chirping away.

The doctor had permitted his release from the hospital under the condition that he went straight home and stayed there. He was not to do anything that required any kind of physical activity. The doctor said this as he looked at her. She blushed slightly; she realized what he meant.

He would report to physical therapy in one week. His left arm and leg were still in a cast, so they would concentrate for now on his lungs. He felt much stronger every day. It was good to be out of the hospital and even better to be here with her. A warm feeling crept through him.

They pulled into his apartment complex. He wasn't surprised to see his supervisor standing next to the entrance. He had suspected there would be a welcoming committee on his arrival. His supervisor helped him out of the car. They all walked up to the apartment. The sidewalk was starting to form a thin sheet of ice so they moved cautiously.

When they finally got inside, he was greeted by his fellow agents. None of them got up or offered any help. It was their way of saying he was still part of an active team. He was handed a glass of wine, and a toast was given on his behalf. His team members stood up. Some of his close friends took turns jokingly giving him advice on how to milk the system. Others told him to quit faking it and get his ass back to work. It was getting kind of late and, as if on cue, they all said their goodbyes and left. Each one promised to check in on him. Soon he was alone with her and his supervisor.

"Are you getting tired?"

"A little." With help from the two of them, he moved slowly to the bedroom.

"Guess I will leave you two alone," said his supervisor. He turned and said, "Call me if you need anything."

She walked him to the door. "There are a lot of people who care about that young man in there. So don't try to do everything by yourself."

"I'll call you if we need anything. Thanks a lot."

"I'll check in day to day. Bye now." He closed the door behind him.

She went back to the bedroom and found him fast asleep. His face was relaxed, sleeping like an angel. He was a good man. She knew the minute she first saw him that he was the one for her. She planned on keeping him. She tiptoed out of the bedroom into the kitchen. She was exhausted. She had spent the past ten days in the hospital. She wanted to lie down and take a long overdue nap, but before she could do that, she decided she should fix something for them to eat. She didn't have time to do any grocery shopping. She had thrown out most of the items in his fridge that morning.

When she opened the refrigerator, she was almost brought to tears. The wives of the men had made food. There were casseroles, beef stews, meatballs, a homemade cake, and several pies. The fridge was overflowing with fruits and vegetables, soft drinks, milk, and juice. A short note was attached to a large chocolate cake, saying that they hoped the two of them would enjoy the food, and that they all would stop by later in the week to check on them.

"There are some terrific people in this world."

She checked on him one last time before she laid down on the couch to get some sleep. Her last nagging thought was of his dad.

I hope he shows up soon.

He rented a small room in the town just outside of his old duty station. There was no private bathroom; the showers and toilets were down the hall. The bed was a single twin that stood guard over a small dresser. A small desk and chair completed the room's spartan furnishings. He rented the room for one week, just enough time to complete his mission. There were still a few things he needed to buy. He sat down at the desk and began to make a list. He knew the town well enough to find everything he needed.

He departed the motel, list in hand, as evening covered the city. The winter's mix of rain and sleet seemed to be racing the falling temperature. The last of the sun's dying rays gave up and retreated to renew its attack on some other part of the world. He walked down the sidewalk thinking about how he once walked this very way with his wife and son enjoying the strange new sights and sounds. The small streets of Bad Tolz held a continuous row of neat shops. He passed a wine vendor handing out free samples. A large pot of wine was being heated with a propane flame. Spirals of steam swirled, and the aroma of the cheap wine filled the air. They had sipped the bittersweet taste years before in another life, when the world was as it should be, before she died.

He stopped abruptly. He rubbed his forehead achingly. He wanted to stop those memories from revisiting him.

"Are you all right, sir?" He looked up and came face to face with a young man and his wife. He saw a baby stroller and inside, bundled in bright blue blankets, was a boy.

"I'm fa. . . . fine. Thank . . . thank you," he replied. "Just a migraine." He would have to be careful not to make a spectacle of himself.

He decided to move on and get some things on his list. He purchased a roll of wire and tape at one store and bought several other household items from another. He bought several batteries and then headed back to his room.

He spent the remainder of the night cooking chemicals on a hot plate. The window was open, so most of the toxic fumes escaped. The brisk night air sent a chill through the room. A heavy snowfall would be coming soon. He was wrapped in a blanket. He used the sheets to cover the cracks in the door and ventilation system. The down pillow kept the chemicals warm. He had to stop periodically and leave the room. The fumes irritated his nose. He stood outside on the sidewalk and breathed deeply. His lungs sent a sickening pain surging through him. His chest hurt with each breath. He coughed nonstop. He went back to his room.

By the time the suns rays had rediscovered his window, he was fast asleep. A long night of mixing chemicals had paid off. Beside the bed was a homemade bomb. It was capable of causing enough damage to shut down the relay station which supplied electrical power to the duty station and this small German town. After some sleep, he went out to find the other items on his list. He purchased a computer and printer.

That evening he paid to hold his room for several more days. He left instructions that he was not to be disturbed by anyone. He hid his bomb and materials in case the maid paid no attention to the "Do not disturb" sign on the door. He left to get something to eat. He walked to a small diner and went over his plan. He thought of all the contingencies and alternative backup plans for each one. He wasn't worried about overlooking something. Twenty years of training had instilled in him the ability to plan a mission from beginning to end with no loose strings. They had trained him well.

CHAPTER 30

The smell made him stir. For a brief moment he forgot that he was injured. He tried to turn over. A sharp, sickening pain pierced his side. The smell of coffee and bacon emanated from the kitchen. He tried to shift to a more comfortable position. His lungs gasped for air. He couldn't take very deep breaths. Sometimes his lungs forced him to inhale deeply. A nauseating sickness reverberated in his stomach. The raw linings in his lungs were repairing themselves. He glanced outside his window. There was a blanket of fresh snow on the ground. A red bird was hopping lightly on top of the powdery flakes looking for food.

She came in with a breakfast tray. His eyes were fixed upon on her, delighting in her smile. She must have been up for several hours he reasoned.

"Hey, gorgeous."

"Hi, handsome. Breakfast is ready. Are you hungry?" He wrapped his arm around her waist and pulled her closer to him.

"That's what woke me up. Right now I don't think food is my main priority."

"You know what the doctor said," she reminded him. "I'm not about to have that old doctor looking down his glasses at me, insinuating that I'm the cause of your maladies. Now eat."

He did eat. The meal was one of the best he had in a long time. She had prepared him a huge ham and cheese omelet, fried potatoes, and crispy bacon with toast and strawberry preserves. He didn't think he could eat all that food, but in no time it was gone.

They shared a cup of coffee together. The phone rang. She handed him the phone. "It's your dad's neighbors," she said nervously.

He took the phone and greeted them. "Yeah, I'm fine. . . . No, I haven't heard from dad. . . . Thank you for putting the fire out. . . . No, I don't need anything. . . . Yes, I'll call as soon as I hear anything. . . . Yeah. . . . I'll come to visit when I can. . . . Thanks for calling." He listened quietly for a few minutes and hung up with a soft and warm goodbye.

His mood had changed. Wonder where pops is hiding out?

She took the dishes to the kitchen and placed them in the dishwasher. She poured another cup of coffee and headed back to the bedroom. She was almost there when there was a knock on the door. Looking through the peep hole she could see his supervisor and several other men standing in the hallway. She opened the door, and they filed in.

"Honey! Get my gun!" She was relieved they had showed up when they did. Anything to take his mind off his father.

"What have you got in those boxes?"

"Your computer," said his supervisor. "Now that you're out of the hospital, its time you get back to work!" The men began to set up his computer. They placed the computer on a night stand beside the bed so the keyboard fit on his lap.

"There you go," said his supervisor, "Now turn it on and plug in your password. You're ready to keep up on the latest events around the world."

She poured them all a cup of coffee. They sat quietly until it dawned on her she was the reason for the uncomfortable silence. She excused herself saying, "Yell if you need more coffee."

She was almost asleep when the men came out of the bedroom with their empty coffee cups. They said their goodbyes, and she headed back to the bedroom. She lay down beside him and put her arm around him.

"Tired?"

"A little," she replied.

"You know, I've been thinking lately that you have been spending too much time worrying about me. You've been at that hospital day and night for almost two solid weeks. While I've just had to lie around like an old hound dog and rest, you've been sleeping in a chair."

He brought out the set of wedding rings he bought a month ago. He was about to ask her to marry him when he heard a soft, rhythmic snore coming softly to his ears.

The train was taking him to Stuttgart, the European equivalent of Fort Bragg. It was the center for all Special Forces missions. He had been there numerous times in his capacity as the NCO in charge of the nuclear arsenal. One thing a soldier learns quickly in all branches of the military is the undeniable fact that shit rolls down hill. Should a unit do poorly on a training mission, the officer may get a stern lecture from his superior. The NCOs may have a counseling statement placed in their permanent records that may affect their chance of getting promoted. When his time was almost up as a drill instructor he submitted the required paperwork complete, with physical, to his company commander requesting Special Forces training.

After a month had gone by, he asked his company commander about the status of his request. His commander, a graduate of West Point and recently assigned to his company, informed him that he had denied his request and had thrown his paper in the trash. His justification was that he knew a few of his friends who had applied and washed out of the course. Therefore he did not think he should waste the government's money to send him.

Normally this would have been the end of discussion, but a friend of his worked at the Department of the Army. He called him and was told to send a copy of his request. Within thirty days, his request had come down through the chain of command with approval.

The reason, of course, was that his friend had asked a general to approve it. No one would disagree with a general. His commander called him into his office and chewed him out for bypassing the chain of command. Reluctantly, he signed off on the approval. He knew this didn't work often in Special Forces, but with just a little twist of luck, he might pull off the most difficult portion of his plan.

Wearing his colonel's uniform, he walked into the main complex in Stuttgart and was not challenged by the security guard. A friendly wave of his hand, and he walked through the gate. The rank on his shoulder and his hurried demeanor was enough to get him past the one specialist on duty behind the desk. The soldier knew he was supposed to challenge anyone who did not have a picture card identification pinned on his or her pocket, but the colonel appeared to be in a hurry and had probably forgotten to put it on. After giving him a greeting, he went back to reading his magazine. Today was Friday. In less than half an hour he would be off duty. No need to cause a fuss.

He continued to the commanding general's office. He was greeted by a very pretty secretary who spoke with a slight German accent.

"Good afternoon, colonel! How may I help you?"

"I'm sorry to trouble you, but my fax machine is broken, and I need to send this message off immediately. May I use yours?"

"Of course you may. Do you want me to send it for you, or can you operate the machine yourself?"

"Thank you, but I don't want to impose any further on your kindness." His pre-typed message was addressed to the commander of Special Forces in Bad Tolz, and he now had the letterhead. Thanks to the politeness of the secretary, he had a cover sheet with the commander of special operations as an authentic heading. The secretary was placing a few items in her purse, getting ready to leave for the weekend when he received confirmation on his fax. He thanked her again and departed the office.

He was exiting the building as the door to the commanding general's door opened. "Have a good weekend, sir!"

"You do the same!" He replied in a pleasant and dignified tone.

He planned for the message to reach headquarters of his old unit just as everyone was leaving for the weekend. The duty officer in charge would notify the battalion commander of its contents. If he had any plans, they would have to be canceled: "A colonel who will identify himself to you on reaching your destination has been sent from Washington, D.C., to inspect the arsenal under your supervision. Please be available on his estimated time of arrival of 2200 hours the evening of November 1st. The inspection will encompass a visual and serial numbered item check of all classified weaponry."

He knew from personal experience that this type of inspection came several times a year infrequently. His research confirmed that the battalion commander was nearing the end of his tour. He himself had to undergo several of these inspections in the past. It had been several years since he had been directly involved in the process, but he felt fairly confident that nothing had changed. The military didn't like to change things as long as the operation ran smoothly.

The battalion commander and the executive officer were waiting in the duty office when he arrived. After introductions and a little small talk, the battalion commander led him down the stairs. The executive officer trailed several steps behind him. After declining the stairs to the lowest level, the battalion commander entered the four-digit code that opened the barred doors. A roving camera recorded the movements of each individual. He stood so each sweep of the camera shot only the back of his head. They continued on to the massive door that secured the atomic bombs. The commander entered a series of coded numbers into the lock. The executive officer took his position and placed his key in the slot marked XO. As soon as the lock was opened, a light flashed above the door. The battalion commander placed his key in the slot, and on the fourth flash both men turned their keys simultaneously. The massive door swung open without making a sound. The three men entered one of the most secure areas in Germany.

He pulled out a stun gun and zapped the battalion commander. The executive officer was turning around when he knocked him down and zapped him. With both men out, he tied their hands securely with their shoelaces. He gagged each of them with their socks.

He picked up his suitcase and took his time going up the stairs. His breath came in irregular short gasps followed by a burning sensation in his lungs. Finally he reached the top. He had to stop and rest while he coughed up bloody mucus.

After regaining his composure, he stopped by the staff duty office. He didn't stay very long, just long enough to zap the young captain and his driver with an extra stun gun. He tied them up the same way he had the other two men. He placed the officer inside a small latrine and the young driver in a utility closet.

He went into the commander's office and located the hidden compartment. He had installed it years ago. He withdrew the cassette tape.

I did a good job installing that, he thought. Walking casually to his rented car, he waved warmly to the guard who saluted him as he drove out the gate. He knew the men he had tied up would be found when the next duty officer reported in. By that time he planned to be far away.

As a little extra insurance, he drove to the relay station which provided the electricity for the military post. He got out of the car and placed a small package on the fence that surrounded the station. He secured it to the fence with the aid of some wire coat hangers. He took his time aiming his device at the transformers. His homemade bomb would detonate at the same time as the new duty officer would come on duty. With luck it might give him several extra hours of time. He waited a few seconds to ensure the timer was working correctly before driving away.

The German police would investigate the explosion and blame one of the many local anti-government groups that survived the aftermath of the Cold War. His bomb was made exactly like one he had recovered and studied intensely when he was stationed here years ago.

Driving over 130 miles an hour on the autobahn did not even raise an eyebrow from the German police. Like all German citizens, they take a great deal of pride in the unrestricted speed limit allowed on their highways.

The next morning he boarded a military aircraft headed for the United States. He explained to the inspectors that he was a courier with top secret documents. No one was permitted to search his rather large briefcase. That also ensured he would fly as number one priority. He was guaranteed a seat on the first plane available. In less than five hours, he had infiltrated a restricted area, secured his bomb, and he was now leaving Frankfort airspace.

The eight-hour flight to New York went smoothly and without incident. He slept most of the way or pretended to be asleep to avoid any conversation. He arrived in New York and was ushered through customs without so much as a glance. He was leaving the airport in his rental car when an alarm went off inside the airport. The intercom was booming throughout the terminal in a very authoritarian voice, "Effective immediately, all military personnel will remain in the terminal until further notice."

He drove to the outskirts of New York and stopped long enough to buy and change into civilian clothes. He drove around Port Jervis until he located a post office. He bought a box and packed his uniform inside, then he mailed it to his home address. He located a men's store and purchased another suit. This he would wear on the final day of his mission. He spent the remainder of the day driving slowly through the lightly falling snow. Jet lag set in, and the effects of living primarily on adrenaline began to wear him down. He pulled into a motel. After four hours of sleep, he woke and was back on the road within fifteen minutes.

They would be looking for him. He had not left much for the authorities to go by, but it would not take them long before they tracked him down. The snow was falling more heavily now. The traffic had slowed to almost a crawl. He spent six hours traveling under thirty miles an hour. He started to nod off. There was a truck stop a few miles down the road. He was less than a hundred miles from Fayetteville, North Carolina. At the truck stop he veered off the exit and pulled in next to the semis. The diesel engines of the big trucks hummed softly in his ears. He closed his eyes and dozed off.

The rays of the cold sun on his frosted window woke him. The traffic on the highway had increased. It was rush hour. The snow had let up; it was a bright, cheerful day. He listened to the radio and, as he expected, there was nothing in the news about his activities. The public wouldn't be notified of his actions. It would only cause a panic if it leaked out.

He was hungry. The truck stop diner was moderately busy. He decided to take a chance and spend some time in the public eye. He walked in and ordered breakfast.

He took the time to shave and put on a clean shirt in the men's room. A short hour and a half later, he was driving into Fayetteville. He felt a little more alert as he drove past the airport. He was glad to see several cars pulling into the parking lot ahead of him. He drove past the airport and proceeded for about ten miles before turning around. He located a family department store and bought a canteen, a backpack, four candy bars, and a small packet of beef jerky.

He pulled into the driveway of the familiar house. He noticed the rundown condition of the front porch. He had done some carpentry work for the old man years ago with his son. They added a new bathroom and rebuilt his back patio. In exchange, the old man had donated his time so they could get certified on a multi-engine plane. He hoped the old man still had the plane.

He knocked on the front door. Inside he heard someone rustling around. "Just a minute." Sounded like him.

The door opened and the old pilot looked him up and down for a few seconds before saying, "Good thing you showed up. I was just getting ready to call the better business bureau and report your shoddy workmanship! Come on in! Come in!"

He accepted the cup of coffee offered, and the two of them sat at the kitchen table getting caught up on old times. "I'm sorry about your wife. I meant to call, but I didn't really know what to say. She must have been a wonderful woman," he said. A sad suffering captured his face.

The old man changed the subject, "How's the boy doing? I haven't seen him in years. Is he . . . " The same stony brace enveloped his entire body and once again the old man knew he said the wrong thing. "I'm sorry. That's . . ." He stopped talking, and they sat silently for a few minutes.

"So what brings you out on such a dreary day?"

"I want to rent your plane for a couple of weeks. I just need some air time and space to clear my head." The old pilot stared at him, trying to read his thoughts. He was a veteran of the Korean and Vietnam wars. He could read men fairly accurately. He knew he had to be convincing, or the old man would be suspicious.

"I just lost my son. He was killed on the job working for the FBI. Now that he and my wife are both gone, I have no one. I want to fly down to Florida and maybe go on over to California. I'd like to visit some of my old Army buddies. Then maybe I'll stop by Vegas. I've never seen it, and I want to take in the night life. I've got to get away from here and from the memories." The old man bought it. He had lost his wife some years back and knew about loneliness.

"So you want to take my plane to relive some of the memories you and your son shared in it, is that it?"

He shook his head. The old pilot stared at him some more. Then he got up and poured them another cup of coffee. "Well, I guess it would be alright if you took old Betty up," he said. "I haven't had her out very much this year. Just had her overhauled and inspected two months ago. She'll give you a good dependable ride."

He shuffled into the kitchen and returned with the keys to his hanger and the plane. "Let her warm up real good before going aloft. When do you plan on leaving?"

"Just as soon as the weather permits."

"You know I wouldn't loan my plane to anyone with the exception of you and your son, don't you?" The old man continued, "I was very fond of that boy. He would have made something in this world." The old pilot rattled off a few more instructions on the operation of the plane before they said their goodbyes.

He pulled out of the driveway and was very glad things had gone this way. He liked the old man and would have disliked killing him to get the keys. The airport wasn't far. He took his backpack and suitcase directly to the plane's hanger. After a thorough inspection, he started the twin engines and let them warm up. He then checked the instruments. He taxied over to the fuel supply point and shut the engines off. The line service tech filled the plane.

The lineman, a young man in his early twenties said, "You're not going up today are you, mister? There's a front coming in bringing freezing rain and sleet."

He assured the lineman, "I'm just taking her up for a few short laps around the field. I'll be back in less than half an hour. I'm thinking about buying the plane, and I wanted to fly her first. Don't worry, I'll be good to ol' Betty."

"Well, you be careful and stay below 3000 feet. The weather around here can be real unforgiving."

"Well, thanks."

He went into the office and paid his fuel bill. The woman behind the desk gave him his change and the same advice. Within minutes, he was lined up on the runway, giving the Baron full throttle. He reached his airspeed and pulled back on the yoke and rotated. He lowered the nose and climbed. Soon he was cruising at 3000 feet. He reached over and flipped the transponder switch off. No need to let them know exactly where he was headed. He was airborne and on the final leg of his journey. It was a trip that would take him to his death and hopefully, the death of the some of the injustice in America. He didn't want to kill all of America, just the part that allowed murderers to go free. This country must suffer for allowing such things to happen and for allowing people to believe they were free, equal, and protected.

He was never allowed to feel equal until he was old enough to kill for his country. He was never allowed to feel free until he killed for his country. Now, when he needed his country the most, the law had been cast aside. His life and his family were destroyed.

He rechecked his gauges. He estimated he had enough fuel to reach his destination and complete his mission. He would have to fly low to keep off the radar.

The ideal location would be in the center of the United States at thirty thousand feet where he could detonate the bomb. An electromagnetic pulse would ripple throughout the continent. It would disable anything that had a computer chip. Planes would drop out of the sky, cars would stop running, electricity wouldn't flow, televisions and radios would become useless. People would panic. The government would be incapable of supplying them with any information. There would widespread crime overnight. The weak and timid would die. At the first sign of hunger, the fighting would begin. There'd be widespread looting and uncontrollable mobs. Vigilantes and militias of neighbors would form to fight and bring about a system of justice. Curfews, hangings, and firing squads would become normal. Judges who passed soft sentences on criminals would have no effect on the new rules. By the time things began to return to normal, America would see the need for making the punishment fit the crime. His plane didn't carry enough fuel to reach the center of the continent. He would fly as far as he could go and then, at the last possible minute, climb to thirty thousand feet. Hopefully he could reach St. Louis or a little farther west before he would climb to his end.

"Now if the weather will just hold out."

CHAPTER 32

He was under an improvised lean-to. A limb was tied horizontally between two trees. He placed smaller branches and leaves over the lean-to to make a waterproof ceiling. His fire burned under the edge of the roof. He heard a slight hissing. The fire ate the attacking drops of rain and defeated it.

The freezing rain had been coming down in a slow drizzle for three days. He was caught in the storm, and he was forced to turn north in the hopes of skirting it. He had to drop altitude frequently because ice formed on the plane's wings. The storm kept pushing him further and further north. He flew lower and lower; he was using too much fuel. He had to find a place to land. He was near his home when he remembered the airstrip that he and his son had stumbled upon years ago. He hoped he could find it before the storm overtook him. He knew if he landed at any airport they would catch him. Every police department in the nation had been alerted. He followed the highway to his hometown. He banked left. He flew over the small country store where he and his dad used to trade. It took him several minutes of circling over his old homestead before he located the airstrip. Just in time.

He came in carefully. He'd never landed on an airstrip covered with ice. He wasn't sure what to expect. He gave the bird full flaps and checked his speed. He touched down harder than he would have liked, but it was a short runway. He fought to keep the mains on the ground and the nose up. He taxied to the edge of the woods. Wasn't all that bad! By the time he shut the engine off and retrieved his backpack, the plane was pelted with freezing rain. He knew he couldn't stay in the aluminum bird. He would freeze to death. He needed to build a small fire to keep from freezing. There was no time to camouflage the plane. He doubted that anyone knew about this place.

He took his gear and walked several miles into the forest before he found an ideal camping spot. There was a small stream flowing between a steep ravine. He would have water, and the ravine walls would protect him from the wind. He was hungry. He hadn't had anything to eat but candy bars and beef jerky in the past two days. He would stay there until tomorrow. He would have to remove the ice from the plane.

He made several trips to the aircraft and covered it with dead limbs and brush. It might be another two days before he could get back in the air. The country store was a good ten miles from his plane. He would leave in the morning; by then the sleet would have stopped. He had enough wood inside his lean-to for the night. He lay down on his bed of pine needles and slept.

The sun shifted its gaze over the horizon. In another half-hour it would be full daylight. The smoke from his fire spiraled in a thin column. The sleet had stopped, but it remained below thirty degrees.

The forest had a spirit of its own. It's a living, breathing city of many different lives and spirits. He was never alone in the forest. He spent years playing in this forest with these spirits. But today the spirits were not with him.

He fashioned a pair of snowshoes from some small saplings. He didn't know if it would snow.

The wood spirits compelled him to tell his neighbors to prepare for hard times. He wouldn't have to tell them everything, just to pack a few items and get lots of food, go to the cabin they owned in the mountains, and stay there until everything returned to normal. They might call the police, but he'd be dead by the time they could trace his call. He thought this might appease the wood spirits. Perhaps they would walk with him now, but they stayed away from him. He was alone on his trek to the store. He walked ten miles through the snow. The woods hadn't changed.

He felt the urge to warn the old couple grow stronger. They were the only people he would feel sorry for when the world turned upside down. His wife would want that. She was very fond of the old couple. He made up his mind. He would call them and tell them to stock up with plenty of food and water. He'd tell them to take everything and go to their cabin. He would caution the old man to get several guns and plenty of ammunition. They would want to know what was going on. He would not tell them. If they heeded his advice, they might live. If not, well, he tried.

He paused at the very edge of the wood. He squatted, resting on his heels. The store was a quarter of a mile in front of him. There were several pickup trucks in the parking lot, nothing to indicate the presence of any outsiders. He checked his wallet. He had very little cash. "I will have to use the credit card."

He moved along the dirt road towards the store. He bought several canned goods and, on the spur of the moment, threw in a coffeepot and coffee. He went outside to the pay phone and called his old friends.

"Hello?" The old man answered on the third ring.

"How are you doing, old timer?"

"My God! My God! Is this really you?" The old man yelled into the phone. "Where in the hell have you been? Do you know how worried we are? Why haven't you called? Do you realize your son has been worried sick about you?"

She pulled him in and softly kissed him. She promised him she would be back tomorrow morning. She had to attend a wedding with her parents. She had to pick up a few things from her apartment. He watched through the bedroom window as she drove off. He was glad to have a few minutes alone to think. Where in the hell was his dad? He called everyone. No one had seen or heard from him. His thoughts were interrupted by a knock at the door. He recognized his supervisor's voice. He could tell by the look on his face that something was wrong.

"Let me hear it." Dread came over him.

His supervisor sat down beside him. He let out a long deep sigh. "There's some news concerning your father. An atomic bomb was stolen from a military base in Germany. The details of how it was accomplished are a little fuzzy right now. The military insists on doing their own investigation."

Slowly his supervisor began to lay out the information available to him. The details of the steps taken in stealing the bomb assured everyone it had to be an inside job, or someone who knew the procedures. "Your dad worked in this area before he retired?"

He nodded his head, and his supervisor went on, "He rented a motel room in the town just off the military base. They found traces of chemicals in the room that matched the bomb that had been detonated at the electrical relay station. It caused a lot of confusion and gave him enough time to get away."

"Any number of people could've done this. Why point the finger at my dad?" There was an edge in his voice. His heart began to race.

His boss moved the chair closer to him. "The forensic inspection of the room produced a small bit of a cigarette filter. We just got it back from the lab. It's the one piece of evidence we have, and the military wanted to put a rush on it. It's a perfect DNA match, and it's a Raleigh cigarette, the same kind your dad smokes. The physical description matches your father. I'm sorry. I think your dad may be going after the Saudi guy who shot you. And I'm convinced he thinks you're dead. Why he needs a bomb like this escapes me, unless he's planning on doing as much damage to that country as possible. I've already alerted the bureau. Have you got any ideas?"

He slowly shook his head. He had a sinking feeling in the depth of his heart. His stomach tied around itself in knots. "What could be the maximum damage this bomb could do?"

"It could easily destroy a city the size of New York. If it were aerially detonated, it could shut down the entire country in a matter of minutes. The blast would fry everything. Planes would fall out of the sky, all electrical plants would stop, and even the cars and trucks would die. You name it, and it probably won't work. No communication systems could operate. Food distribution and manufacturing would stop. People would starve. Hospitals would shut down. It would be a nightmare."

He assured his supervisor he would call him if he heard anything from his dad.

"I'm going to have a trace put on your phone. Let's hope he calls so we can stop him before he does something horrible. I'm sorry to give you this kind of news, kid. I'll have the trace on your phone installed first thing in the morning. If you should hear from him before then, let me know ASAP."

He was left alone with his thoughts. Would his dad go so far as to bomb another country? It was not the Saudis Arabian's fault that he had been shot. Who did his dad blame? His mother's killer getting off on such a light sentence had disappointed them both. His dad thought he was dead, therefore what would he do or who would he blame? If his dad had taken that bomb, would he go so far as to declare war on another country? He might kill the guy who had shot him. He did not think he would destroy another country; it wasn't their fault.

No, he wasn't going after Saudi Arabia. Those people created enough misery for themselves. Why kill them? So where would he direct the blame? His mom's killer got off because of our laws, his dad had said on several occasions. Now his dad thought he was dead. Would that be enough for him to want to hurt or get even with the United States? That's it! He wants this country to pay!

A sudden thought came to him. The two of them had learned to fly together. I wonder, he said aloud as he began typing in his password on his computer. In a matter of a few minutes the information was staring at him on the screen. There was nothing indicating a plane had been stolen.

His fingers glided sweatily over the keys. How high does a plane have to be to cause the most possible damage with a bomb? He searched the reference index for the information: thirty thousand feet. Who did his father know that had a plane? There was only one man, an old pilot who gave them flying lessons. What was his name? He couldn't remember his last name. He raked through his papers but he couldn't find a trace of it. All he knew was that the airport was in Fayetteville.

It didn't take him long to track the old pilot down. The old man answered the phone on the fourth ring. "Hello."

"Hello, sir. I doubt if you remember me. My dad and I did some repair work on your house a long time ago in exchange for some flying lessons."

The old man swore and then said, "I had a feeling your dad wasn't telling me the truth." A cold feeling came over him. He didn't need to ask any more questions. He knew his father had the bomb. Worse still, he also knew his dad had a plane.

He laid there, sweat formed on his forehead. He forgot all about the pain he was in and desperately tried to put the puzzle together. This was his father, for crying out loud. Could he really have done such a heinous crime? In his heart he knew his dad was capable of doing inhuman things to survive. He never discussed his time in the Special Forces. His father had not been in his right frame of mind since his mother's death. It was plausible that he could go off the deep end.

His thoughts turned slowly to the whereabouts of the missing plane, thinking about where it could be hidden. His dad had taken off just in front of a storm front. Did he crash? No, that was not likely, because someone would have reported a plane crash. If he landed at an air strip he would have been discovered by now. Where could he land? More importantly where could he land and feel safe? It had to be a remote location where he would not be easily recognized. He had to land in a place he knew, but where he didn't fear people knowing him or observing him or hearing the plane. The answer slowly came to him as he put the pieces of the puzzle together.

He knew in his heart that his dad had the plane. His dad had the bomb. His dad did not intend to use it on any foreign country. No, he planned on seeking revenge on the country that killed his wife and son. This was the country that had stripped him of his pride and hurt him many times in the past. The same country had now taken everything from him in the present. He was going to destroy this country!

Forcing himself to think, he recalled the camping trip when he and his dad had made a visit to his father's boyhood home. The vision he had from his grandfather! The words sounding like airstrip as his voice faded away. That's it! The airstrip the two of them found! He felt a shiver go through him. Had his grandfather known about this all those years ago?

It was all falling into place now. How much time did he have? Should he call his supervisor? How could he tell him without proof? Would he pull valuable men and resources that were working around the clock on his hunch? What if he was wrong?

He slid out of bed and retrieved his crutches. He hobbled to the garage and found a disc sander. He started removing the cast on his leg. When he was done, he went back to his bedroom and struggled with his hiking boots. He was dressed and ready to leave. He scribbled a short message and left it on the phone. He paused as he passed the gun cabinet. He took out his deer rifle and loaded it with the 30-06 shells.

It was only eleven o'clock in the morning. If he drove the rest of the day and all night he might get to his destination in time to stop his father. He was pulling out of the driveway when the phone in his apartment began to ring. Had he been there, he may have even felt the nervous energy from the caller before he picked it up.

His dad left a message that made little sense except that he loved him and would see him very soon. His voice cracked as he expressed his surprise and joy to find his boy was alive. His dad kept talking on the answering machine until the time ran out.

CHAPTER 34

The throbbing anguish of his injured leg sent waves of pain through his nervous system. Spasm after spasm seized his lungs. His heart pounded. Both injuries were trying to force him down. Thankfully, he had less than thirty miles to go. He kept going over the possible location of the airstrip. The one and only time he had been near it, he was only sixteen years old. He remembered it was due east of their campsite. He pushed all thoughts of his father's justifications and tried to stay focused on reaching the airstrip. How far was it from their campsite? How long would it take him to find it in his condition? Time was of the essence. He had to get there before the plane took off. The weather played a factor too. Tomorrow the skies would be clear. Daylight was just about to break as he pulled onto the old dirt road. There were no signs of any vehicles or tire tracks. The place didn't appear to have seen any form of human life.

The road was covered with small saplings and scrub brush. After one mile, the dense undergrowth made it impossible for him to drive any farther. He got out of the car and stood for a few minutes trying to get his bearings. The campsite would be off somewhere to his left if his memory was correct.

The day they discovered the airstrip it was early in the afternoon. On the trip back to the camp the sun was in his eyes. They must have traveled east. He waited a few more minutes, searching his memory for any telltale sign of the direction. Nothing else came to mind, so he decided to go with his first impression. With a feeling of unknown dread, he pulled the gun out and checked the chamber and safety. He started his slow walk in an easterly direction. The exertion of the walk made him gasp for air. The raw linings of his lungs refused to accept the frigid burning sensation caused by breathing.

The sun was showing its full face. It covered the wooded area with erratic rays of warmth. Dancing patterns of light reflected through icicles suspended from the trees. He didn't notice how beautiful they were. He was too busy to listen to the wood spirits. He moved slower on his crutch. He was determined to find his father. Had this been under any other circumstances, he would have given up, but his dad's life depended on this. He would have to find the airstrip and stop the plane from getting off the ground. He forced each step. They became increasingly more difficult and painful. But he didn't notice. He was preoccupied and didn't see the glistening icicles. He ignored their sultry dance steps. They beckoned him to play, to change his mind, to turn around.

She entered the apartment with her key. "Are you hungry?" She expected to hear a loud positive grunt. The silence that answered sent a chill down her spine. Something was wrong.

She walked slowly into the bedroom. Her eyes took in the unmade bed. There were dirty dishes sitting on the tray stand. A note was placed on the phone where she would be sure to see it. She picked up the paper with a shaking hand and read with disbelief. "Honey, I had to leave. I think my dad is up to something. I have to stop him before he gets hurt. I'll call you as soon as I can. I love you."

The answering machine had two new messages. She pressed play and almost fainted when she recognized his father's voice. "Son . . . I just found out you were alive." There was a moment of silence. "I will be flying in tomorrow. Everything will be ok."

There was more silence followed by blaring beep of the machine. The second message was from the neighbors. The old man's voice was loud and excited. He had just heard from his dad. Had he talked to him yet? The noise of the old woman could be heard in the background coming through loud and clear as she cried and praised the Lord at the same time. The old man continued to talk until the phone recorder shut off.

She saved both messages. She dialed his cell phone. The phone rang and rang. And it continued to ring as it rested on the car seat. The only person who could have answered it was almost two miles away, sitting on a tree stump, his body shaking from physical weakness and mental anguish.

A severe spell of coughing brought up bloody phlegm that left him weak and cold. He was still happy though. His son was alive. He could withstand anything now because his son was alive. His old neighbor had told him of his boy's wounds and his health. He was home recuperating. He was all right. He was all right. He smiled, wiping the sweat from his forehead, relieved. He called to his son's house, but the answering machine picked up. He left a short message then held on, willing his son to pick up the phone. When he did not do so, he hung up with regret at not getting to hear the boy's voice. His walk back to camp was one of mixed emotions.

It had been daylight for almost an hour when his coughing shook him from a deep sleep. He got up and set the coffeepot on the coals to warm the liquid. He reached into his shirt pocket and removed his last cigarette. He lit it, a smile coming over his face as the tobacco smoke refused to go down his lungs. After several painful coughs he put the butt out. "Well, sweetheart, guess this is a good time to quit."

He grabbed the coffeepot and poured a cup. Now if he could just get the plane up without crashing. He had never taken off on a runway covered in ice. If he couldn't take off, he would walk back to the store and catch a ride into town. He wasn't going to risk crashing and dying now. Not now that he had a chance to see his son's face once more.

He glared at the briefcase inside the lean-to. Strange how something which just several hours earlier had seemed to be the answer to his problems now turned into Goliath—only problems.

"Fate sure played you a funny hand this time." He took out a pen and paper. He had several dreams in the past few days that he wanted to write down. At first he couldn't understand them, but his son's rebirth was beginning to make sense. He would give them to his son to read after he was gone. From the amount of pain and discomfort his chest had been giving him lately, he knew he didn't have much time left. If he crashed on take-off, his son would have this letter.

The sun, with help from the shadows, reminded him it was nine o'clock. It was time to go. He brushed snow into the fire with his boot and looked around the campsite. There was nothing he needed to take with him but the letter and the suitcase.

He laid there in pure agony. The cold from the frozen ground seeped through his clothing. He had fallen. His injured leg was caught in a tree root. It had thrown him headfirst down a steep slope. He had been excited. He hadn't been looking. All he had seen was the plane. He must have passed out; he couldn't remember anything else. His chest hurt. The fall had slammed him to the ground hard. He tried to take a deep breath but felt a stabbing pain go through his body.

He began to crawl up the slope. If he could reach the crest of the hill, he could see the plane. He prayed that it was really there and that it hadn't been just his imagination. It took him almost thirty minutes to reach the top. It was there! The camouflage had been removed; someone was walking around the craft giving it a pre-flight inspection. He couldn't make out the features of the man but he knew who he was.

"Dad!" He yelled, but his voice was just above a whisper. He looked around for his crutch. It was lying near the bottom of the hill. He knew he couldn't go down and retrieve it. He didn't have the strength or the time.

He pulled the rifle from his back and looked through the scope. There was no question about it, that was his dad. The plane's engine was running. His dad finished the pre-flight inspection. He was moving towards the door. He had to stop him. He aimed at his father's leg. He would just wound him so that he couldn't fly. His dad turned and scanned the trees in his direction.

Just as he pulled the trigger, his father dived to the ground. He watched in horror as the bullet caught his father just above his left eye. His dad teetered for a few seconds before falling to the ground. Throwing the rifle down, he began to crawl. He had to reach his dad. All thoughts of pain and fatigue were forgotten. He dragged his useless leg behind him. He had one thought, to save his dad's life—if he were still alive.

"Please God. Please God."

CHAPTER 38

1999 He awoke to the sound of gentle scraping. He pulled on his pants and got out of his sleeping bag. His dad was squatting Indian-style, removing the last traces of flesh from a deer. Lately his dad had him going on hunting trips that would last several days. His father was working on something back at the camp. He would tan the deer hides when he was away. On the ground was a large bag stuffed with hides. The one his father was working on tediously was the last of their recent hunt. He walked over to the fire and poured himself a cup of coffee. The smoke from the fire went straight up in a thin blue gray column.

"No rain today," he said out loud. He glanced over at his father. He wondered how he was feeling this morning. The scar from the bullet was still purplish. The surgeons had done an excellent job saving his life. The damage to his brain had been severe. It had left his dad without the ability to speak. He stood up and stretched. His dad pointed to the bow and arrows leaning against a tree. Then he pointed to the deerskin in front of him.

"Already?" he said. His dad nodded yes and pointed to the woods.

"Ok, you old fart," he said. He stuffed a knapsack full of deer jerky and a canteen of water. He gave his dad a warm hug, picked up the bow and arrows, and headed for the woods. Whenever he asked his dad what he was doing with so many skins, he'd shrug and continue what he was doing. He kept the skins he finished in a large bag. He made it clear that the boy wasn't permitted to look inside.

It was late in the fall but still some time before deer season would begin. They were on their family's land. His dad was dying. If a few illegal deerskins made him happy, he was not going to deny him. He moved silently through the woods thinking about the last time he was here.

Somehow he had managed to crawl 300 yards to his dad. He had ripped off his shirt and made a crude bandage to stop the blood flow. He had wrestled himself inside the aircraft and radioed for help. A rescue chopper was there within the hour. They loaded his dad onto a stretcher and rushed him off to the hospital. He gave the medical personnel the number to his supervisor's office with instructions to tell them he had the suitcase they were looking for.

On the medical crew's insistence, they left one man with him. The warm blankets and hot coffee revived him. He didn't want any painkillers or drugs. He was more afraid of losing the bomb than losing his leg. The EMT fretted over it. He finally got the blood to stop flowing. He was light-headed from loss of blood but held onto his senses. They waited a long time before he heard the distant noise of helicopters.

The choppers touched down, and his supervisor and a team of three other men came toward him. After retrieving the suitcase, his supervisor motioned for the emergency crew. They loaded him onto the chopper. He tried to convey a message to his supervisor who interrupted his stuttered speech and assured him he would call her.

He passed out shortly after that. He couldn't remember the ride or arriving at the hospital. He woke briefly as the doctor yanked his broken leg back into place. Late the following day, he was wheeled into the room where his father was. He ordered the nursing staff to place his bed next to his dad's. He had held his dad's hand through the night.

His thoughts were broken as his eyes fell on a fresh set of deer tracks.

CHAPTER 39

He was more than ready for his crossing, but he had one more thing to do. His determination to finish this project was stronger than the cancer eating him. The deer hides were now tanned. He had to cut and sew them. He could only do it when his son was asleep or away. He smiled, his final gift. He couldn't give his son very much in this world, but he could give him this. His body was wasted. He was ready to go. His only regret was leaving his boy.

He smiled to himself as he thought of his boy spending the night somewhere out there in the deep woods. Good for him. It's time away from the daily grind of watching me waste away. No man had a finer son. His heart swelled with pride. No man could ask for more than what he had at this very moment.

The fire had died to a glow of soft red embers. The stars were calling to him. It wouldn't be much longer. The sound of a whippoorwill came a short distance from the trees. He forced himself to sit up. He reached for the bag where he kept the deerskins he was working on. He began kneading them. He rubbed deer brains into the hide with his hands.

After his recovery, he was given a military hearing. He expected to spend the rest of his life in prison, which wouldn't be that long. The president of the United States intervened. He put a stop to any military or civilian trial. His term in office constantly bounced from one scandal to another. He was not about to bring to the public's attention that a nuclear bomb had been stolen on his watch. He called in the FBI director, the top military brass, the CIA. He informed them that if this got out to the papers there would be more than just his bloody testicles on the chopping block. He told them to give the son of a bitch whatever would make him happy to keep him quiet until he died.

A deal was offered to him in exchange for revealing all the steps he had taken to steal the bomb. If he disclosed everything, he could live on his remote property until his death.

There were two more conditions for his release: He was not permitted to seek medical help, and he had to wear an ankle bracelet for as long as he lived. He would have a limited supply of medication for his pain. There would be no doctors or any outside contacts other than his immediate family.

He didn't have to think about the proposition. He merely pointed to the computer. His plan had been simple down to the last detail. After his confession was complete, the military took measures to ensure it could never happen again. He was released into his son's custody, and a military escort saw them arrive at his present location. The military had a small contingent of soldiers guarding the perimeter just in case. The guards were given orders to observe but not interfere with the two men.

The battalion commander and the executive officer had been permitted to retire. The sergeant who gave him an identification card without the proper paper work had been demoted to private. The sergeant who issued him a passport had been demoted to the rank of specialist and was now serving in Alaska. The store clerk who sold him a uniform without checking his ID had been promoted. Now she was in charge of ordering all military supplies including officers' uniforms. There was a solemn-looking older woman working for the general of special operations command in Europe. The younger, prettier one was transferred to another department. She was given a pay raise with more responsibility outside of the military complex. He was thankful that no one was truly damaged beyond repair.

The whippoorwill began his singing again. It brought him to a much happier time, a time far away where there was a warm, loving mother and a strong father, a time when he was special, a time when he was the center of their universe. His pain was forgotten as he continued his work. The glow from the fire cast an eerie shadow across his sunken face, yet his eyes were bright with warmth. Last night he had a wonderful dream. He had seen a little blonde-haired boy running around his mother collecting Easter eggs.

She made her way through the woods. A small path had formed where she walked on her weekly visits. The twelve-hour drive left so little time to spend with the two of them. The Special Forces soldiers greeted her in a quiet, respectful manner. They always asked to inspect her backpack. She didn't know where they were staying, but she knew they maintained constant surveillance on the campsite. They would intercept her each time she made her trip but never in the same location. She couldn't help but feel a small amount of dread as she approached the campsite. The initial shock of seeing the changes in both men filled her with dread.

As she struggled up a small incline, she recalled how close she had come to losing both of them. Thankfully he stayed in the hospital just a few weeks before he was given permission to go home.

A small tug of guilt pulled at her conscience. For as long as the two of them would be together, she would have a terrible secret she must keep from him. If he knew about the messages, it would have killed him. Had he been aware of the two telephone calls, he wouldn't have been compelled to shoot his dad. Thanks to his supervisor and the promise of his old neighbors, he would never find out. The phone recorder had been replaced with a new one. The old one was placed safely in FBI files where he would never see it.

The FBI had given him permanent disability. He drew a portion of his check each month. It wouldn't be enough for them to live on, not in a large city. His meager wage would barely pay for the rent and leave nothing for food or other necessities. She dreaded the time when he would start looking for a job.

For the time being, they were here. They were safe and together. There was something special about this place. She couldn't put it into words. There was a comfort all around the forest that seemed to grow on her. It called to her a little more each time she came to visit. True, she always felt a deep sadness when she had to leave her two men. But over time, the truth slowly came to her. This feels like home. She, a big city girl, was slowly turning into a country bumpkin! The forest had a healing effect on her soul. The birds and squirrels greeted her. She couldn't help but breathe in the beauty and peacefulness of this place. A yellow bird flew nearby and landed softly on a small branch. The happy creature turned his head and chirped hello to her. The golden leaves fell gracefully from the trees. The sunlight filtered through the canopy of oaks. She stopped to take in the vast landscape of art before her. Stay . . . stay . . . the forest seemed to whisper.

Her boyfriend would stay here until the end came, to look after his dad. She was thankful to have them both together. She would do everything she could to talk him into another career, any job that didn't involve law enforcement or anything that dangerous. She wanted to see him come home safely every night. Her parents had offered him a job, but she didn't think he could adjust to such a boring life.

She was almost there. She could smell the smoke from the campfire. She came to the small clearing and was alarmed to find it empty. He had pitched a tent for her. The campsite was neat and clean. She took off her small backpack. She brought coffee, sugar, soup, and a bag of flour. She eased it to the ground. She looked around at the forest. She found the trail she knew she would have to take someday. She began to run. A feeling of dread swept over her. In her heart, she knew she was too late.

She found him at the grave site. She made her way to his side. She placed her arm around his waist and stood there. There were seven graves now: his great-grandparents', his grandparents', his aunt's, his mother's, and his father's. Her thoughts were filled with an alternate past, one in which the four of them could have laughed and played through a life without turmoil or disease.

As the evening sun began to gasp its last breath, the two of them walked back to the campsite. He let go of her hand and crawled inside the lean-to. He returned with a bundle that was wrapped in a waterproof bag made of deer skin.

"This is a gift for you and me," he said choking back his tears. "Dad's last wish was for the two of us to open this together. This is the last thing he could give us from his Indian heritage. He gave it to us with all his heart. He said to tell you he loves you and is so happy to have been blessed with knowing you."

CHAPTER 41

They stood in front of the Blackfoot medicine man as he blessed the two of them in marriage. Her parents and friends were standing along with his fellow co-workers and close friends from the FBI. His adopted grandma and grandpa arrived the night before. There were many tears and hugs as the four of them spent the night talking about the two people now gone. She had never met his mother, and the stories were all that she would know. We would have been best friends, she thought to herself.

The day was bright and clear. There were large rolling clouds covering a turquoise sky. A slight breeze wrapped around them in their happiness. The old couple stood holding hands in the place where his parents would've have stood. The ceremony didn't last long. They were dressed in bleached white deerskin, complete with moccasins. The beads and porcupine quills that decorated her white dress showed the time and care he had put into it. She had a moment of sadness thinking of his dad struggling to finish the traditional Indian dress. He had worked on it up to the night he died. I wish he could see me now. She glanced up at her husband. He looked so handsome in his white buckskins. Like a warrior, she thought, a man who belonged in another time, another era.

They received congratulations and hugs from their friends. Her mind began to wander and daydream. While they had looked after his day, they had talked about the future. Although both of them loved the city, the peacefulness and tranquility of this place had grown within each of them. Slowly, they had come to love this land with all its wild animals and streams. They had become a part of this place. They were entwined with the stars and dust. She inhaled deeply the fresh, clean air. There were memories here from the past that called to the living. There was a tranquility surrounding the mountain that brought comfort. A feeling of belonging captured her heart. She felt the invisible hands of love guide and protect her on this patch of earth.

They would live here and raise a family. They would never be rich, but they would have a wealth in what really mattered—time for each other and time for a family.

She had found the ideal place for playing games with their children—a very old and large oak tree. It had wide, majestic limbs for climbing or for a swing. There was plenty of shade and soft, lush moss to lay and roll around in. A small cool stream ran nearby. It bubbled as it tumbled over rocks. It was the place to play hide and seek, or just cuddle telling stories. She had spent many hours lying in the plush moss with her husband, staring at the clouds. As she walked beside him, her mind continued to daydream of all the possibilities of this special place.

A thought came to her as they walked arm in arm together. It sent chills through her. She couldn't wait to start a family.

"What a perfect place for hiding Easter eggs!"